Outstanding Contemporary Plays
in SIGNET Editions

The American Dream

AND

The Zoo Story

TWO PLAYS BY EDWARD ALBEE

A SIGNET BOOK from

NEW AMERICAN LIBRARY

TIMES MIRROR

Published as a SIGNET BOOK
by arrangement with Coward-McCann, Inc.,
who have authorized this softcover edition.
Hardcover editions are available from Coward-McCann, Inc.

THIRTEENTH PRINTING

Ⓢ SIGNET TRADEMARK REG. U.S. PAT. OFF. AND FOREIGN COUNTRIES
REGISTERED TRADEMARK—MARCA REGISTRADA
HECHO EN CHICAGO, U.S.A.

SIGNET, SIGNET CLASSICS, SIGNETTE, MENTOR AND PLUME BOOKS
are published by The New American Library, Inc.,
1301 Avenue of the Americas, New York, New York 10019

PRINTED IN THE UNITED STATES OF AMERICA

The Zoo Story

A PLAY IN ONE SCENE (1958)

For William Flanagan

PREFACE

With the exception of a three-act sex farce I composed when I was twelve—the action of which occurred aboard an ocean liner, the characters of which were, for the most part, English gentry, and the title of which was, for some reason that escapes me now, *Aliqueen*—with the exception of that, *The Zoo Story* (1958), *The Death of Bessie Smith* and *The Sandbox* (both 1959), are my first three plays.

The Zoo Story, written first, received production first—but not in the United States, where one might reasonably expect an American writer to get his first attention. *The Zoo Story* had its première in Berlin, Germany, on September 28, 1959. How it got to production so shortly after it was written, and how, especially, it got to Berlin, might be of interest—perhaps to point up the Unusual, the Unlikely, the Unexpected, which, with the exception of the fare the commercial theatre setup spills out on its dogged audience each season, is the nature of the theatre.

Shortly after *The Zoo Story* was completed, and while it was being read and politely refused by a number of New York producers (which was not to be unexpected, for no one at all had ever heard of its author, and it *was* a short play, and short plays *are,* unfortunately, anathema to producers and—supposedly—to audiences), a young composer friend of mine, William Flanagan by name, looked at the play, liked it, and sent it to several friends of his, among them David Diamond, another American composer, resident in Italy; Diamond liked the play and sent it on to a friend of *his,* a Swiss actor, Pinkas Braun; Braun liked the play, made a tape recording of it, playing both its roles, which he sent on to Mrs. Stefani Hunzinger, who heads the drama department of the S. Fischer Verlag, a large publishing house in Frankfurt; she, in turn . . . well, through her it got to Berlin, and to production. From New York to Florence to Zurich to Frankfurt to Berlin. And finally back to New York where, on January 14, 1960, it received American production, off Broadway, at the Provincetown Playhouse, on a double bill with Samuel Beckett's *Krapp's Last Tape.*

I went to Berlin for the opening of *The Zoo Story.* I had not planned to—it seemed like such a distance, such an expense—but enough friends said to me that, of course, I would be present at the first performance of my first play, that I found myself, quickly enough, replying, yes, yes, of course; I wouldn't miss it for the world. And so, I went; and I *wouldn't* have missed it for the world. I wouldn't have missed it for the world, despite the fact—as I have learned since—that, for this author, at least, opening nights do not really exist. They happen, but they take place as if in a dream: One concentrates, but one cannot see the stage action clearly; one can hear but barely; one tries to follow the play, but one can make no sense of it. And, if one is called to the stage afterwards to take a bow, one wonders why, for one can make no connection between the work just presented and one's self. Naturally, this feeling was complicated in the case of *The Zoo Story,* as the play was being presented in German, a language of which I knew not a word, and in Berlin, too, an awesome city. But, it has held true since. The high points of a person's life can be appreciated so often only in retrospect.

The Death of Bessie Smith also had its première in Berlin, while *The Sandbox* was done first in New York.

The Sandbox, which is fourteen minutes long, was written to satisfy a commission from the Festival of Two Worlds for a short dramatic piece for the Festival's summer program in Spoleto, Italy—where it was not performed. I was, at the time of the commission, at work on a rather longer play, *The American Dream,* which I subsequently put aside and have, at this writing, just taken up again. For *The Sandbox,* I extracted several of the characters from *The American Dream* and placed them in a situation different than, but related to, their predicament in the longer play. They seem happy out of doors, in *The Sandbox,* and I hope they will not be distressed back in a stuffy apartment, in *The American Dream.*

Along with *The American Dream,* I am at various stages of writing, or thinking about, three other plays: two other less-than-full-evening ones—*Bedlam* and *The Substitute Speaker* (this a working title)—and a full-evening play, *The Exorcism,* or: *Who's Afraid of Virginia Woolf.*

Careers are funny things. They begin mysteriously and, just as mysteriously, they can end; and I am at just the very beginning of what I hope will be a long and satisfying life in the theatre. But, whatever happens, I am grateful to have had my novice work received so well, and so soon.

EDWARD ALBEE

New York City
July 4, 1960

FIRST PERFORMANCE: September 28, 1959.
Berlin, Germany.

Schiller Theater Werkstatt.

FIRST AMERICAN PERFORMANCE: January 14, 1960.
New York City.

The Provincetown Playhouse.

The Zoo Story

The Players:

PETER: A man in his early forties, neither fat nor gaunt, neither handsome nor homely. He wears tweeds, smokes a pipe, carries horn-rimmed glasses. Although he is moving into middle age, his dress and his manner would suggest a man younger.

JERRY: A man in his late thirties, not poorly dressed, but carelessly. What was once a trim and lightly muscled body has begun to go to fat; and while he is no longer handsome, it is evident that he once was. His fall from physical grace should not suggest debauchery; he has, to come closest to it, a great weariness.

The Scene:

It is Central Park; a Sunday afternoon in summer; the present. There are two park benches, one toward either side of the stage; they both face the audience. Behind them: foliage, trees, sky. At the beginning, Peter is seated on one of the benches.

Stage Directions:

As the curtain rises, PETER *is seated on the bench stage-right. He is reading a book. He stops reading, cleans his glasses, goes back to reading.* JERRY *enters.*

JERRY

I've been to the zoo. (PETER *doesn't notice*) I said, I've been to the zoo. MISTER, I'VE BEEN TO THE ZOO!

PETER

Hm? . . . What? . . . I'm sorry, were you talking to me?

JERRY

I went to the zoo, and then I walked until I came here. Have I been walking north?

PETER (*Puzzled*)

North? Why . . . I . . . I think so. Let me see.

JERRY

(*Pointing past the audience*) Is that Fifth Avenue?

PETER

Why yes; yes, it is.

JERRY

And what is that cross street there; that one, to the right?

PETER

That? Oh, that's Seventy-fourth Street.

JERRY

And the zoo is around Sixty-fifth Street; so, I've been walking north.

PETER

(*Anxious to get back to his reading*) Yes; it would seem so.

JERRY

Good old north.

PETER

(*Lightly, by reflex*) Ha, ha.

JERRY

(*After a slight pause*) But not due north.

PETER

I . . . well, no, not due north; but, we . . . call it north.
It's northerly.

JERRY

(*Watches as* PETER, *anxious to dismiss him, prepares
his pipe*) Well, boy; *you're* not going to get lung cancer,
are you?

PETER

(*Looks up, a little annoyed, then smiles*) No, sir. Not
from this.

JERRY

No, sir. What you'll probably get is cancer of the mouth,
and then you'll have to wear one of those things Freud
wore after they took one whole side of his jaw away.
What do they call those things?

PETER (*Uncomfortable*)

A prosthesis?

JERRY

The very thing! A prosthesis. You're an educated man,
aren't you? Are you a doctor?

PETER

Oh, no; no. I read about it somewhere; *Time* magazine,
I think. (*He turns to his book*)

JERRY

Well, *Time* magazine isn't for blockheads.

PETER

No, I suppose not.

JERRY

(*After a pause*) Boy, I'm glad that's Fifth Avenue there.

PETER (*Vaguely*)

Yes.

JERRY

I don't like the west side of the park much.

PETER

Oh? (*Then, slightly wary, but interested*) Why?

JERRY (*Offhand*)

I don't know.

PETER

Oh. (*He returns to his book*)

JERRY

(*He stands for a few seconds, looking at* PETER, *who finally looks up again, puzzled*) Do you mind if we talk?

PETER

(*Obviously minding*) Why . . . no, no.

JERRY

Yes you do; you do.

PETER

(*Puts his book down, his pipe out and away, smiling*) No, really; I don't mind.

JERRY

Yes you do.

PETER

(*Finally decided*) No; I don't mind at all, really.

JERRY

It's . . . it's a nice day.

PETER

(*Stares unnecessarily at the sky*) Yes. Yes, it is; lovely.

JERRY

I've been to the zoo.

PETER

Yes, I think you said so . . . didn't you?

JERRY

You'll read about it in the papers tomorrow, if you don't see it on your TV tonight. You have TV, haven't you?

PETER

Why yes, we have two; one for the children.

JERRY

You're married!

PETER

(*With pleased emphasis*) Why, certainly.

JERRY

It isn't a law, for God's sake.

PETER

No . . . no, of course not.

JERRY

And you have a wife.

PETER

(*Bewildered by the seeming lack of communication*) Yes!

JERRY

And you have children.

PETER

Yes; two.

JERRY

Boys?

PETER

No, girls . . . both girls.

JERRY

But you wanted boys.

PETER

Well . . . naturally, every man wants a son, but . . .

JERRY

(*Lightly mocking*) But that's the way the cookie crumbles?

PETER (*Annoyed*)

I wasn't going to say that.

JERRY

And you're not going to have any more kids, are you?

PETER

(*A bit distantly*) No. No more. (*Then back, and irksome*) Why did you say that? How would you know about that?

JERRY

The way you cross your legs, perhaps; something in the voice. Or maybe I'm just guessing. Is it your wife?

PETER (*Furious*)

That's none of your business! (*A silence*) Do you understand? (JERRY *nods.* PETER *is quiet now*) Well, you're right. We'll have no more children.

JERRY (*Softly*)

That *is* the way the cookie crumbles.

PETER (*Forgiving*)

Yes . . . I guess so.

JERRY

Well, now; what else?

PETER

What were you saying about the zoo . . . that I'd read about it, or see . . . ?

JERRY

I'll tell you about it, soon. Do you mind if I ask you questions?

PETER

Oh, not really.

JERRY

I'll tell you why I do it; I don't talk to many people—except to say like: give me a beer, or where's the john, or what time does the feature go on, or keep your hands to yourself, buddy. You know—things like that.

PETER

I must say I don't . . .

JERRY

But every once in a while I like to talk to somebody, really *talk;* like to get to know somebody, know all about him.

PETER

(*Lightly laughing, still a little uncomfortable*) And am I the guinea pig for today?

JERRY

On a sun-drenched Sunday afternoon like this? Who better than a nice married man with two daughters and . . . uh . . . a dog? (PETER *shakes his head*) No? Two dogs. (PETER *shakes his head again*) Hm. No dogs?

(PETER *shakes his head, sadly*) Oh, that's a shame. But
you look like an animal man. CATS? (PETER *nods his
head, ruefully*) Cats! But, that can't be your idea. No,
sir. Your wife and daughters? (PETER *nods his head*)
Is there anything else I should know?

PETER

(*He has to clear his throat*) There are . . . there are two
parakeets. One . . . uh . . . one for each of my daughters.

JERRY

Birds.

PETER

My daughters keep them in a cage in their bedroom.

JERRY

Do they carry disease? The birds.

PETER

I don't believe so.

JERRY

That's too bad. If they did you could set them loose in
the house and the cats could eat them and die, maybe.
(PETER *looks blank for a moment, then laughs*) And
what else? What do you do to support your enormous
household?

PETER

I . . . uh . . . I have an executive position with a . . . a
small publishing house. We . . . uh . . . we publish text-
books.

JERRY

That sounds nice; very nice. What do you make?

PETER (*Still cheerful*)

Now look here!

JERRY

Oh, come on.

PETER

Well, I make around eighteen thousand a year, but I don't carry more than forty dollars at any one time . . . in case you're a . . . a holdup man . . . ha, ha, ha.

JERRY

(*Ignoring the above*) Where do you live? (PETER *is reluctant*) Oh, look; I'm not going to rob you, and I'm not going to kidnap your parakeets, your cats, or your daughters.

PETER (*Too loud*)

I live between Lexington and Third Avenue, on Seventy-fourth Street.

JERRY

That wasn't so hard, was it?

PETER

I didn't mean to seem . . . ah . . . it's that you don't really carry on a conversation; you just ask questions. and I'm , . . I'm normally . . . . uh . . . reticent. Why do you just stand there?

JERRY

I'll start walking around in a little while, and eventually I'll sit down. (*Recalling*) Wait until you see the expression on his face.

PETER

What? Whose face? Look here; is this something about the zoo?

JERRY (*Distantly*)

The what?

PETER

The zoo; the zoo. Something about the zoo.

JERRY

The zoo?

PETER

You've mentioned it several times.

JERRY

(*Still distant, but returning abruptly*) The zoo? Oh, yes; the zoo. I was there before I came here. I told you that. Say, what's the dividing line between upper-middle-middle-class and lower-upper-middle-class?

PETER

My dear fellow, I...

JERRY

Don't my dear fellow me.

PETER (*Unhappily*)

Was I patronizing? I believe I was; I'm sorry. But, you see, your question about the classes bewildered me.

JERRY

And when you're bewildered you become patronizing?

PETER

I ... I don't express myself too well, sometimes. (*He attempts a joke on himself*) I'm in publishing, not writing.

JERRY

(*Amused, but not at the humor*) So be it. The truth is· I was being patronizing.

PETER

Oh, now; you needn't say that.

(*It is at this point that Jerry may begin to*

move about the stage with slowly increasing determination and authority, but pacing himself, so that the long speech about the dog comes at the high point of the arc)

JERRY

All right. Who are your favorite writers? Baudelaire and J. P. Marquand?

PETER *(Wary)*

Well, I like a great many writers; I have a considerable . . . catholicity of taste, if I may say so. Those two men are fine, each in his way. *(Warming up)* Baudelaire, of course . . . uh . . . is by far the finer of the two, but Marquand has a place . . . in our . . . uh . . . national . . .

JERRY

Skip it.

PETER

I . . . sorry.

JERRY

Do you know what I did before I went to the zoo today? I walked all the way up Fifth Avenue from Washington Square; all the way.

PETER

Oh; you live in the Village! *(This seems to enlighten* PETER)

JERRY

No, I don't. I took the subway down to the Village so I could walk all the way up Fifth Avenue to the zoo. It's one of those things a person has to do; sometimes a person has to go a very long distance out of his way to come back a short distance correctly.

PETER *(Almost pouting)*

Oh, I thought you lived in the Village.

JERRY

What were you trying to do? Make sense out of things? Bring order? The old pigeonhole bit? Well, that's easy; I'll tell you. I live in a four-story brownstone rooming-house on the upper West Side between Columbus Avenue and Central Park West. I live on the top floor; rear; west. It's a laughably small room, and one of my walls is made of beaverboard; this beaverboard separates my room from another laughably small room, so I assume that the two rooms were once one room, a small room, but not necessarily laughable. The room beyond my beaverboard wall is occupied by a colored queen who always keeps his door open; well, not always, but *always* when he's plucking his eyebrows, which he does with Buddhist concentration. This colored queen has rotten teeth, which is rare, and he has a Japanese kimono, which is also pretty rare; and he wears this kimono to and from the john in the hall, which is pretty frequent. I mean, he goes to the john a lot. He never bothers me, and he never brings anyone up to his room. All he does is pluck his eyebrows, wear his kimono and go to the john. Now, the two front rooms on my floor are a little larger, I guess; but they're pretty small, too. There's a Puerto Rican family in one of them, a husband, a wife, and some kids; I don't know how many. These people entertain a lot. And in the other front room, there's somebody living there, but I don't know who it is. I've never seen who it is. Never. Never ever.

PETER (*Embarrassed*)

Why . . . why do you live there?

JERRY

(*From a distance again*) I don't know.

PETER

It doesn't sound like a very nice place . . . where you live.

JERRY

Well, no; it isn't an apartment in the East Seventies. But, then again, I don't have one wife, two daughters, two cats and two parakeets. What I do have, I have toilet articles, a few clothes, a hot plate that I'm not supposed to have, a can opener, one that works with a key, you know; a knife, two forks, and two spoons, one small, one large; three plates, a cup, a saucer, a drinking glass, two picture frames, both empty, eight or nine books, a pack of pornographic playing cards, regular deck, an old Western Union typewriter that prints nothing but capital letters, and a small strongbox without a lock which has in it . . . what? Rocks! Some rocks . . . sea-rounded rocks I picked up on the beach when I was a kid. Under which . . . weighed down . . . are some letters . . . please letters . . . please why don't you do this, and please when will you do that letters. And when letters, too. When will you write? When will you come? When? These letters are from more recent years.

PETER

(*Stares glumly at his shoes, then*) About those two empty picture frames . . . ?

JERRY

I don't see why they need any explanation at all. Isn't it clear? I don't have pictures of anyone to put in them.

PETER

Your parents . . . perhaps . . . a girl friend . . .

JERRY

You're a very sweet man, and you're possessed of a truly enviable innocence. But good old Mom and good old Pop are dead . . . you know? . . . I'm broken up about it, too . . . I mean really. BUT. That particular vaudeville act is playing the cloud circuit now, so I don't see how I can look at them, all neat and framed. Besides, or, rather, to be pointed about it, good old Mom walked out on good old Pop when I was ten and a half

years old; she embarked on an adulterous turn of our
southern states . . . a journey of a year's duration . . .
and her most constant companion . . . among others,
among many others . . . was a Mr. Barleycorn. At least,
that's what good old Pop told me after he went down
. . . came back . . . brought her body north. We'd received the news between Christmas and New Year's, you
see, that good old Mom had parted with the ghost in
some dump in Alabama. And, without the ghost . . . she
was less welcome. I mean, what was she? A stiff . . . a
northern stiff. At any rate, good old Pop celebrated the
New Year for an even two weeks and then slapped into
the front of a somewhat moving city omnibus, which
sort of cleaned things out family-wise. Well no; then
there was Mom's sister, who was given neither to sin nor
the consolations of the bottle. I moved in on her, and my
memory of her is slight excepting I remember still that
she did all things dourly: sleeping, eating, working, pray-
ing. She dropped dead on the stairs to her apartment, my
apartment then, too, on the afternoon of my high school
graduation. A terribly middle-European joke, if you ask
me.

PETER

Oh, my; oh, my.

JERRY

Oh, your what? But that was a long time ago, and I have
no feeling about any of it that I care to admit to myself.
Perhaps you can see, though, why good old Mom and
good old Pop are frameless. What's your name? Your
first name?

PETER

I'm Peter.

JERRY

I'd forgotten to ask you. I'm Jerry.

PETER

(*With a slight, nervous laugh*) Hello, Jerry.

JERRY

(*Nods his hello*) And let's see now; what's the point of having a girl's picture, especially in two frames? I have two picture frames, you remember. I never see the pretty little ladies more than once, and most of them wouldn't be caught in the same room with a camera. It's odd, and I wonder if it's sad.

PETER

The girls?

JERRY

No. I wonder if it's sad that I never see the little ladies more than once. I've never been able to have sex with, or, how is it put? . . . make love to anybody more than once. Once; that's it. . . . Oh, wait; for a week and a half, when I was fifteen . . . and I hang my head in shame that puberty was late . . . I was a h-o-m-o-s-e-x-u-a-l. I mean, I was queer . . . (*Very fast*) . . . queer, queer, queer . . . with bells ringing, banners snapping in the wind. And for those eleven days, I met at least twice a day with the park superintendent's son . . . a Greek boy, whose birthday was the same as mine, except he was a year older. I think I was very much in love . . . maybe just with sex. But that was the jazz of a very special hotel, wasn't it? And now; oh, do I love the little ladies; really, I love them. For about an hour.

PETER

Well, it seems perfectly simple to me. . . .

JERRY (*Angry*)

Look! Are you going to tell me to get married and have parakeets?

PETER (*Angry himself*)

Forget the parakeets! And stay single if you want to. It's

no business of mine. I didn't start this conversation in the . . .

JERRY

All right, all right. I'm sorry. All right? You're not angry?

PETER (*Laughing*)

No, I'm not angry.

JERRY (*Relieved*)

Good. (*Now back to his previous tone*) Interesting that you asked me about the picture frames. I would have thought that you would have asked me about the pornographic playing cards.

PETER

(*With a knowing smile*) Oh, I've seen those cards.

JERRY

That's not the point. (*Laughs*) I suppose when you were a kid you and your pals passed them around, or you had a pack of your own.

PETER

Well, I guess a lot of us did.

JERRY

And you threw them away just before you got married.

PETER

Oh, now; look here. I didn't *need* anything like that when I got older.

JERRY

No?

PETER (*Embarrassed*)

I'd rather not talk about these things.

JERRY

So? Don't. Besides, I wasn't trying to plumb your post-adolescent sexual life and hard times; what I wanted to get at is the value difference between pornographic playing cards when you're a kid, and pornographic playing cards when you're older. It's that when you're a kid you use the cards as a substitute for a real experience, and when you're older you use real experience as a substitute for the fantasy. But I imagine you'd rather hear about what happened at the zoo.

PETER (*Enthusiastic*)

Oh, yes; the zoo. (*Then, awkward*) That is . . . if you. . . .

JERRY

Let me tell you about why I went . . . well, let me tell you some things. I've told you about the fourth floor of the roominghouse where I live. I think the rooms are better as you go down, floor by floor. I guess they are; I don't know. I don't know any of the people on the third and second floors. Oh, wait! I do know that there's a lady living on the third floor, in the front. I know because she cries all the time. Whenever I go out or come back in, whenever I pass her door, I always hear her crying, muffled, but . . . very determined. Very determined indeed. But the one I'm getting to, and all about the dog, is the landlady. I don't like to use words that are too harsh in describing people. I don't like to. But the landlady is a fat, ugly, mean, stupid, unwashed, misanthropic, cheap, drunken bag of garbage. And you may have noticed that I very seldom use profanity, so I can't describe her as well as I might.

PETER

You describe her . . . vividly.

JERRY

Well, thanks. Anyway, she has a dog, and I will tell you about the dog, and she and her dog are the gatekeepers of my dwelling. The woman is bad enough; she leans around in the entrance hall, spying to see that I don't bring in things or people, and when she's had her mid-afternoon pint of lemon-flavored gin she always stops me in the hall, and grabs ahold of my coat or my arm, and she presses her disgusting body up against me to keep me in a corner so she can talk to me. The smell of her body and her breath . . . you can't imagine it . . . and somewhere, somewhere in the back of that pea-sized brain of hers, an organ developed just enough to let her eat, drink, and emit, she has some foul parody of sexual desire. And I, Peter, I am the object of her sweaty lust.

PETER

That's disgusting. That's . . . horrible.

JERRY

But I have found a way to keep her off. When she talks to me, when she presses herself to my body and mumbles about her room and how I should come there, I merely say: but, Love; wasn't yesterday enough for you, and the day before? Then she puzzles, she makes slits of her tiny eyes, she sways a little, and then, Peter . . . and it is at this moment that I think I might be doing some good in that tormented house . . . a simple-minded smile begins to form on her unthinkable face, and she giggles and groans as she thinks about yesterday and the day before; as she believes and relives what never happened. Then, she motions to that black monster of a dog she has, and she goes back to her room. And I am safe until our next meeting.

PETER

It's so . . . unthinkable. I find it hard to believe that people such as that really *are*.

JERRY

(*Lightly mocking*) It's for reading about, isn't it?

PETER (*Seriously*)

Yes.

JERRY

And fact is better left to fiction. You're right, Peter.
Well, what I have been meaning to tell you about is the
dog; I shall, now.

PETER (*Nervously*)

Oh, yes; the dog.

JERRY

Don't go. You're not thinking of going, are you?

PETER

Well . . . no, I don't think so.

JERRY

(*As if to a child*) Because after I tell you about the
dog, do you know what then? Then . . . then I'll tell you
about what happened at the zoo.

PETER (*Laughing faintly*)

You're . . . you're full of stories, aren't you?

JERRY

You don't *have* to listen. Nobody is holding you here; remember that. Keep that in your mind.

PETER (*Irritably*)

I know that.

JERRY

You do? Good.
(*The following long speech, it seems to me,
should be done with a great deal of action, to
achieve a hypnotic effect on Peter, and on the
audience, too. Some specific actions have been
suggested, but the director and the actor playing
Jerry might best work it out for themselves*)

ALL RIGHT. (*As if reading from a huge billboard*)
THE STORY OF JERRY AND THE DOG! (*Natural
again*) What I am going to tell you has something to do
with how sometimes it's necessary to go a long distance
out of the way in order to come back a short distance
correctly; or, maybe I only think that it has something
to do with that. But, it's why I went to the zoo today,
and why I walked north . . . northerly, rather . . . until
I came here. All right. The dog, I think I told you, is a
black monster of a beast: an oversized head, tiny, tiny
ears, and eyes . . . bloodshot, infected, maybe; and a
body you can see the ribs through the skin. The dog is
black, all black; all black except for the bloodshot eyes,
and . . . yes . . . and an open sore on its . . . *right* fore-
paw; that is red, too. And, oh yes; the poor monster, and
I do believe it's an old dog . . . it's certainly a misused
one . . . almost always has an erection . . . of sorts.
That's red, too. And . . . what else? . . . oh, yes; there's
a gray-yellow-white color, too, when he bares his fangs.
Like this: Grrrrrrr! Which is what he did when he saw
me for the first time . . . the day I moved in. I worried
about that animal the very first minute I met him. Now,
animals don't take to me like Saint Francis had birds
hanging off him all the time. What I mean is: animals
are indifferent to me . . . like people (*He smiles slightly*)
. . . most of the time. But this dog wasn't indifferent.
From the very beginning he'd snarl and then go for me,
to get one of my legs. Not like he was rabid, you know;
he was sort of a stumbly dog, but he wasn't half-assed,
either. It was a good, stumbly run; but I always got
away. He got a piece of my trouser leg, look, you can
see right here, where it's mended; he got that the second day I lived there; but, I kicked free and got upstairs
fast, so that was that. (*Puzzles*) I still don't know to
this day how the other roomers manage it, but you know
what I *think:* I think it had to do only with me. Cozy.
So. Anyway, this went on for over a week, whenever I
came in; but never when I went out. That's funny. Or,
it *was* funny. I could pack up and live in the street for all
the dog cared. Well, I thought about it up in my room

one day, one of the times after I'd bolted upstairs, and I made up my mind. I decided: First, I'll kill the dog with kindness, and if that doesn't work . . . I'll just kill him. (PETER *winces*) Don't react, Peter; just listen. So, the next day I went out and bought a bag of hamburgers, medium rare, no catsup, no onion; and on the way home I threw away all the rolls and kept just the meat.

(*Action for the following, perhaps*)

When I got back to the roominghouse the dog was waiting for me. I half opened the door that led into the entrance hall, and there he was; waiting for me. It figured. I went in, very cautiously, and I had the hamburgers, you remember; I opened the bag, and I set the meat down about twelve feet from where the dog was snarling at me. Like so! He snarled; stopped snarling; sniffed; moved slowly; then faster; then faster toward the meat. Well, when he got to it he stopped, and he looked at me. I smiled; but tentatively, you understand. He turned his face back to the hamburgers, smelled, sniffed some more, and then . . . RRRAAAAGGGGGHHHH, like that . . . he tore into them. It was as if he had never eaten anything in his life before, except like garbage. Which might very well have been the truth. I don't think the landlady ever eats anything but garbage. But. He ate all the hamburgers, almost all at once, making sounds in his throat like a woman. *Then,* when he'd finished the meat, the hamburger, and tried to eat the paper, too, he sat down and smiled. I think he smiled; I know cats do. It was a very gratifying few moments. Then, BAM, he snarled and made for me again. He didn't get me this time, either. So, I got upstairs, and I lay down on my bed and started to think about the dog again. To be truthful, I was offended, and I was damn mad, too. It was six perfectly good hamburgers with not enough pork in them to make it disgusting. I was offended. But, after a while, I decided to try it for a few more days. If you think about it, this dog had what amounted to an antipathy toward me; really. And, I wondered if I mightn't overcome this antipathy. So, I tried it for five more days, but it was always the same: snarl, sniff; move; faster; stare; gobble; RAAGGGHHH; smile; snarl; BAM. Well, now; by this time Columbus Avenue was strewn with hamburger rolls and I was less offended than disgusted. So, I decided to kill the dog.

(PETER *raises a hand in protest*)

Oh, don't be so alarmed, Peter; I didn't succeed. The day I tried to kill the dog I bought only one hamburger and what I thought was a murderous portion of rat poison. When I bought the hamburger I asked the man not to bother with the roll, all I wanted was the meat. I expected some reaction from him, like: we don't sell no hamburgers without rolls; or, wha' d'ya wanna do, eat it out'a ya han's? But no; he smiled benignly, wrapped up the hamburger in waxed paper, and said: A bite for ya pussy-cat? I wanted to say: No, not really; it's part of a plan to poison a dog I know. But, you can't say "a dog I know" without sounding funny; so I said, a little too loud, I'm afraid, and too formally: YES, A BITE FOR MY PUSSY-CAT. People looked up. It always happens when I try to simplify things; people look up. But that's neither hither nor thither. So. On my way back to the roominghouse, I kneaded the hamburger and the rat poison together between my hands, at that point feeling as much sadness as disgust. I opened the door to the entrance hall, and there the monster was, waiting to take the offering and then jump me. Poor bastard; he never learned that the moment he took to smile before he went for me gave me time enough to get out of range. BUT, there he was; malevolence with an erection, waiting. I put the poison patty down, moved toward the stairs and watched. The poor animal gobbled the food down as usual, smiled, which made me almost sick, and then, BAM. But, I sprinted up the stairs, as usual, and the dog didn't get me, as usual. AND IT CAME TO PASS THAT THE BEAST WAS DEATHLY ILL. I knew this because he no longer attended me, and because the landlady sobered up. She stopped me in the hall the same evening of the attempted murder and confided the information that God had struck her puppy-dog a surely fatal blow. She had forgotten her bewildered lust, and her eyes were wide open for the first time. They looked like the dog's eyes. She sniveled and implored me to pray for the animal. I wanted to say to her: Madam, I have myself to pray for, the colored queen, the Puerto Rican family, the person in the front room whom I've never seen, the woman who cries deliberately behind her closed door, and the rest of the people in all roominghouses, everywhere; besides, Madam, I don't understand how to pray. But . . . to simplify things . . . I told her I would pray. She looked up. She said that I was a liar, and that I probably wanted the dog to die. I told her, and there was so much truth here, that I didn't want the dog to die. I didn't, and not just because I'd poisoned him. I'm afraid that I must tell you I wanted the dog to live so that I could see what our new relationship might come to.

(PETER *indicates his increasing displeasure and slowly growing antagonism*)

Please understand, Peter; that sort of thing is important. You must believe me; it *is* important. We have to know the effect of our actions. (*Another deep sigh*) Well, anyway; the dog recovered. I have no idea why, unless he was a descendant of the puppy that guarded the gates of hell or some such resort. I'm not up on my mythology. (*He pronounces the word myth-o-logy*) Are you?

(PETER *sets to thinking, but* JERRY *goes on*)

At any rate, and you've missed the eight-thousand-dollar question, Peter; at any rate, the dog recovered his health and the landlady recovered her thirst, in no way altered by the bow-wow's deliverance. When I came home from a movie that was playing on Forty-second Street, a movie I'd seen, or one that was very much like one or several I'd seen, after the landlady told me puppykins was better, I was so hoping for the dog to be waiting for me. I was . . . well, how would you put it . . . enticed? . . . fascinated? . . . no, I don't think so . . . heart-shatteringly anxious, that's it; I was heart-shatteringly anxious to confront my friend again.

(PETER *reacts scoffingly*)

Yes, Peter; friend. That's the only word for it. I was heart-shatteringly et cetera to confront my doggy friend again. I came in the door and advanced, unafraid, to the center of the entrance hall. The beast was there . . . looking at me. And, you know, he looked better for his scrape with the nevermind. I stopped; I looked at him; he looked at me. I think . . . I think we stayed a long time that way . . . still, stone-statue . . . just looking at one another. I looked more into his face than he looked into mine. I mean, I can concentrate longer at looking into a dog's face than a dog can concentrate at looking into mine, or into anybody else's face, for that matter. But during that twenty seconds or two hours that we looked into each other's face, we made contact. Now, here is what I had wanted to happen: I loved the dog now, and I wanted him to love me. I had tried to love, and I had tried to kill, and both had been unsuccessful by themselves. I hoped . . . and I don't really know why I expected the dog to understand anything, much less my motivations . . . I hoped that the dog would understand.

(PETER *seems to be hypnotized*)

It's just . . . it's just that . . . (JERRY *is abnormally tense, now*) . . . it's just that if you can't deal with people, you have to make a start somewhere. WITH ANIMALS! (*Much faster now, and like a conspirator*) Don't you see? A person has to have some way of dealing with SOMETHING. If not with people . . . if not with people . . . SOMETHING. With a bed, with a cockroach, with a mirror . . . no, that's too hard, that's one of the last steps. With a cockroach, with a . . . with a . . . with a carpet, a roll of toilet paper . . . no, not that, either . . . that's a mirror, too; always check bleeding. You see how hard it is to find things? With a street corner, and too many lights, all colors reflecting on the oily-wet streets . . . with a wisp of smoke, a wisp . . . of smoke . . . with . . . with pornographic playing cards, with a strongbox . . . WITHOUT A LOCK . . . with love, with vomiting, with crying, with fury because the

pretty little ladies aren't pretty little ladies, with making
money with your body which is an act of love and I
could prove it, with howling because you're alive; with
God. How about that? WITH GOD WHO IS A COL-
ORED QUEEN WHO WEARS A KIMONO AND
PLUCKS HIS EYEBROWS, WHO IS A WOMAN WHO
CRIES WITH DETERMINATION BEHIND HER
CLOSED DOOR . . . with God who, I'm told, turned
his back on the whole thing some time ago . . . with
. . . some day, with people. (JERRY *sighs the next word
heavily*) People. With an idea; a concept. And where
better, where ever better in this humiliating excuse for a
jail, where better to communicate one single, simple-
minded idea than in an entrance hall? Where? It would
be A START! Where better to make a beginning . . .
to understand and just possibly be understood . . . a
beginning of an understanding, than with . . .
> (*Here* JERRY *seems to fall into almost grotesque
> fatigue*)
. . . than with A DOG. Just that; a dog.
> (*Here there is a silence that might be prolonged
> for a moment or so; then* JERRY *wearily finishes
> his story*)
A dog. It seemed like a perfectly sensible idea. Man is a
dog's best friend, remember. So: the dog and I looked at
each other. I longer than the dog. And what I saw then
has been the same ever since. Whenever the dog and I
see each other we both stop where we are. We regard
each other with a mixture of sadness and suspicion, and
then we feign indifference. We walk past each other
safely; we have an understanding. It's very sad, but you'll
have to admit that it is an understanding. We had made
many attempts at contact, and we had failed. The dog
has returned to garbage, and I to solitary but free passage. I have not returned. I mean to say, I have *gained*
solitary free passage, if that much further loss can be
said to be gain. I have learned that neither kindness
nor cruelty by themselves, independent of each other,
creates any effect beyond themselves; and I have learned
that the two combined, together, at the same time, are

the teaching emotion. And what is gained is loss. And what has been the result: the dog and I have attained a compromise; more of a bargain, really. We neither love nor hurt because we do not try to reach each other. And, *was* trying to feed the dog an act of love? And, perhaps, was the dog's attempt to bite me *not* an act of love? If we can so misunderstand, well then, why have we invented the word love in the first place?

> (*There is silence.* JERRY *moves to* PETER'S *bench and sits down beside him. This is the first time* JERRY *has sat down during the play*)

The Story of Jerry and the Dog: the end.

> (PETER *is silent*)

Well, Peter? (JERRY *is suddenly cheerful*) Well, Peter? Do you think I could sell that story to the *Reader's Digest* and make a couple of hundred bucks for *The Most Unforgettable Character I've Ever Met?* Huh?

> (JERRY *is animated, but* PETER *is disturbed*)

Oh, come on now, Peter; tell me what you think.

PETER (*Numb*)

I . . . I don't understand what . . . I don't think I . . . (*Now, almost tearfully*) Why did you tell me all of this?

JERRY

Why not?

PETER

I DON'T UNDERSTAND!

JERRY

(*Furious, but whispering*) That's a lie.

PETER

No. No, it's not.

JERRY (*Quietly*)

I tried to explain it to you as I went along. I went slowly; it all has to do with . . .

PETER

I DON'T WANT TO HEAR ANY MORE. I don't understand you, or your landlady, or her dog. . . .

JERRY

Her dog! I thought it was my . . . No. No, you're right.
It *is* her dog. (*Looks at* PETER *intently, shaking his
head*) I don't know what I was thinking about; of course
you don't understand. (*In a monotone, wearily*) I don't
live in your block; I'm not married to two parakeets, or
whatever your setup is. I am a *permanent transient,* and
my home is the sickening roominghouses on the West
Side of New York City, which is the greatest city in the
world. Amen.

PETER

I'm . . . I'm sorry; I didn't mean to . . .

JERRY

Forget it. I suppose you don't quite know what to make
of me, eh?

PETER (*A joke*)

We get all kinds in publishing. (*Chuckles*)

JERRY

You're a funny man. (*He forces a laugh*) You know
that? You're a very . . . a richly comic person.

PETER

(*Modestly, but amused*) Oh, now, not really. (*Still
chuckling*)

JERRY

Peter, do I annoy you, or confuse you?

PETER (*Lightly*)

Well, I must confess that this wasn't the kind of afternoon I'd anticipated.

JERRY

You mean, I'm not the gentleman you were expecting.

PETER

I wasn't expecting anybody.

JERRY

No, I don't imagine you were. But I'm here, and I'm not leaving.

PETER

(*Consulting his watch*) Well, you may not be, but I must be getting home soon.

JERRY

Oh, come on; stay a while longer.

PETER

I really should get home; you see . . .

JERRY

(*Tickles* PETER's *ribs with his fingers*) Oh, come on.

PETER

    (*He is very ticklish; as* JERRY *continues to tickle him his voice becomes falsetto*)
No, I . . . OHHHHH! Don't do that. Stop, Stop. Ohhh, no, no.

JERRY

Oh, come on.

PETER

(*As* JERRY *tickles*) Oh, hee, hee, hee. I must go. I . . . hee, hee, hee. After all, stop, stop, hee, hee, hee, after all, the parakeets will be getting dinner ready soon. Hee, hee. And the cats are setting the table. Stop, stop, and, and . . . (PETER *is beside himself now*) . . . and we're having . . . hee, hee . . . uh . . . ho, ho, ho.
    (JERRY *stops tickling* PETER, *but the combina-*

tion of the tickling and his own mad whimsy has
PETER *laughing almost hysterically. As his laugh-*
ter continues, then subsides, JERRY *watches him,*
with a curious fixed smile)

JERRY

Peter?

PETER

Oh, ha, ha, ha, ha, ha. What? What?

JERRY

Listen, now.

PETER

Oh, ho, ho. What . . . what is it, Jerry? Oh, my.

JERRY (*Mysteriously*)

Peter, do you want to know what happened at the zoo?

PETER

Ah, ha, ha. The what? Oh, yes; the zoo. Oh, ho, ho. Well,
I had my own zoo there for a moment with . . . hee,
hee, the parakeets getting dinner ready, and the . . . ha,
ha, whatever it was, the . . .

JERRY (*Calmly*)

Yes, that was very funny, Peter. I wouldn't have expected it. But do you want to hear about what happened at the zoo, or not?

PETER

Yes. Yes, by all means; tell me what happened at the
zoo. Oh, my. I don't know what happened to me.

JERRY

Now I'll let you in on what happened at the zoo; but
first, I should tell you why I went to the zoo. I went to
the zoo to find out more about the way people exist
with animals, and the way animals exist with each other,

and with people too. It probably wasn't a fair test, what with everyone separated by bars from everyone else, the animals for the most part from each other, and always the people from the animals. But, if it's a zoo, that's the way it is. (*He pokes* PETER *on the arm*) Move over.

PETER (*Friendly*)
I'm sorry, haven't you enough room? (*He shifts a little*)

JERRY (*Smiling slightly*)
Well, all the animals are there, and all the people are there, and it's Sunday and all the children are there. (*He pokes* PETER *again*) Move over.

PETER
(*Patiently, still friendly*) All right.
          (*He moves some more, and* JERRY *has all the room he might need*)

JERRY
And it's a hot day, so all the stench is there, too, and all the balloon sellers, and all the ice cream sellers, and all the seals are barking, and all the birds are screaming. (*Pokes* PETER *harder*) Move over!

PETER
(*Beginning to be annoyed*) Look here, you have more than enough room! (*But he moves more, and is now fairly cramped at one end of the bench*)

JERRY
And I am there, and it's feeding time at the lions' house, and the lion keeper comes into the lion cage, one of the lion cages, to feed one of the lions. (*Punches* PETER *on the arm, hard*) MOVE OVER!

PETER
(*Very annoyed*) I can't move over any more, and stop hitting me. What's the matter with you?

JERRY

Do you want to hear the story? (*Punches* PETER's *arm again*)

PETER (*Flabbergasted*)

I'm not so sure! I certainly don't want to be punched in the arm.

JERRY

(*Punches* PETER's *arm again*) Like that?

PETER

Stop it! What's the matter with you?

JERRY

I'm crazy, you bastard.

PETER

That isn't funny.

JERRY

Listen to me, Peter. I want this bench. You go sit on the bench over there, and if you're good I'll tell you the rest of the story.

PETER (*Flustered*)

But . . . whatever for? What *is* the matter with you? Besides, I see no reason why I should give up this bench. I sit on this bench almost every Sunday afternoon, in good weather. It's secluded here; there's never anyone sitting here, so I have it all to myself.

JERRY (*Softly*)

Get off this bench, Peter; I want it.

PETER

(*Almost whining*) No.

JERRY

I said I want this bench, and I'm going to have it. Now get over there.

PETER

People can't have everything they want. You should know that; it's a rule; people can have some of the things they want, but they can't have everything.

JERRY (*Laughs*)

Imbecile! You're slow-witted!

PETER

Stop that!

JERRY

You're a vegetable! Go lie down on the ground.

PETER (*Intense*)

Now *you* listen to me. I've put up with you all afternoon.

JERRY

Not really.

PETER

LONG ENOUGH. I've put up with you long enough. I've listened to you because you seemed . . . well, because I thought you wanted to talk to somebody.

JERRY

You put things well; economically, and, yet . . . oh, what is the word I want to put justice to your . . . JESUS, you make me sick . . . get off here and give me my bench.

PETER

MY BENCH!

JERRY

(*Pushes* PETER *almost, but not quite, off the bench*) Get out of my sight.

PETER

(*Regaining his position*) God da . . . mn you. That's enough! I've had enough of you. I will not give up this bench; you can't have it, and that's that. Now, go away.

(JERRY *snorts but does not move*)

Go away, I said.

(JERRY *does not move*)

Get away from here. If you don't move on . . . you're a bum . . . that's what you are. . . . If you don't move on, I'll get a policeman here and make you go.

(JERRY *laughs, stays*)

I warn you, I'll call a policeman.

JERRY (*Softly*)

You won't find a policeman around here; they're all over on the west side of the park chasing fairies down from trees or out of the bushes. That's all they do. That's their function. So scream your head off; it won't do you any good.

PETER

POLICE! I warn you, I'll have you arrested. POLICE! (*Pause*) I said POLICE! (*Pause*) I feel ridiculous.

JERRY

You look ridiculous: a grown man screaming for the police on a bright Sunday afternoon in the park with nobody harming you. If a policeman *did* fill his quota and come sludging over this way he'd probably take you in as a nut.

PETER

(*With disgust and impotence*) Great God, I just came here to read, and now you want me to give up the bench. You're mad.

JERRY

Hey, I got news for you, as they say. I'm on your precious bench, and you're never going to have it for yourself again.

PETER (*Furious*)

Look, you; get off my bench. I don't care if it makes any sense or not. I want this bench to myself; I want you OFF IT!

JERRY (*Mocking*)

Aw . . . look who's mad.

PETER

GET OUT!

JERRY

No.

PETER

I WARN YOU!

JERRY

Do you know how ridiculous you look *now?*

PETER

(*His fury and self-consciousness have possessed him*) It doesn't matter. (*He is almost crying*) GET AWAY FROM MY BENCH!

JERRY

Why? You have everything in the world you want; you've told me about your home, and your family, and *your own* little zoo. You have everything, and now you want this bench. Are these the things men fight for? Tell me, Peter, is this bench, this iron and this wood, is this your honor? Is this the thing in the world you'd fight for? Can you think of anything more absurd?

PETER

Absurd? Look, I'm not going to talk to you about honor, or even try to explain it to you. Besides, it isn't a question of honor; but even if it were, you wouldn't understand.

JERRY (*Contemptuously*)

You don't even know what you're saying, do you? This is probably the first time in your life you've had anything more trying to face than changing your cats' toilet box. Stupid! Don't you have any idea, not even the slightest, what other people *need?*

PETER

Oh, boy, listen to you; well, you don't need this bench. That's for sure.

JERRY

Yes; yes, I do.

PETER (*Quivering*)

I've come here for years; I have hours of great pleasure, great satisfaction, right here. And that's important to a man. I'm a responsible person, and I'm a GROWNUP. This is my bench, and you have no right to take it away from me.

JERRY

Fight for it, then. Defend yourself; defend your bench.

PETER

You've *pushed* me to it. Get up and fight.

JERRY

Like a man?

PETER (*Still angry*)

Yes, like a man, if you insist on mocking me even further.

JERRY

I'll have to give you credit for one thing: you *are* a vegetable, and a slightly nearsighted one, I think . . .

PETER

THAT'S ENOUGH. . . .

JERRY

. . . but, you know, as they say on TV all the time—you know—and I mean this, Peter, you have a certain dignity; it surprises me. . . .

PETER

STOP!

JERRY

(*Rises lazily*) Very well, Peter, we'll battle for the bench, but we're not evenly matched.
  (*He takes out and clicks open an ugly-looking knife*)

PETER

(*Suddenly awakening to the reality of the situation*)
You *are* mad! You're stark raving mad! YOU'RE GOING TO KILL ME!
  (*But before* PETER *has time to think what to do,* JERRY *tosses the knife at* PETER'S *feet*)

JERRY

There you go. Pick it up. You have the knife and we'll be more evenly matched.

PETER (*Horrified*)

No!

JERRY

(*Rushes over to* PETER, *grabs him by the collar;* PETER *rises; their faces almost touch*)
Now you pick up that knife and you fight with me. You fight for your self-respect; you fight for that goddamned bench.

PETER (*Struggling*)

No! Let . . . let go of me! He . . . Help!

JERRY

(*Slaps* PETER *on each "fight"*) You fight, you miserable

bastard; fight for that bench; fight for your parakeets; fight for your cats, fight for your two daughters; fight for your wife; fight for your manhood, you pathetic little vegetable. (*Spits in* PETER's *face*) You couldn't even get your wife with a male child.

PETER
(*Breaks away, enraged*) It's a matter of genetics, not manhood, you . . . you monster.
> (*He darts down, picks up the knife and backs off a little; he is breathing heavily*)

I'll give you one last chance; get out of here and leave me alone!
> (*He holds the knife with a firm arm, but far in front of him, not to attack, but to defend*)

JERRY (*Sighs heavily*)
So be it!
> (*With a rush he charges* PETER *and impales himself on the knife. Tableau: For just a moment, complete silence,* JERRY *impaled on the knife at the end of* PETER's *still firm arm. Then* PETER *screams, pulls away, leaving the knife in* JERRY. JERRY *is motionless, on point. Then he, too, screams, and it must be the sound of an infuriated and fatally wounded animal. With the knife in him, he stumbles back to the bench that* PETER *had vacated. He crumbles there, sitting, facing* PETER, *his eyes wide in agony, his mouth open*)

PETER (*Whispering*)
Oh my God, oh my God, oh my God. . . .
> (*He repeats these words many times, very rapidly*)

JERRY
(JERRY *is dying; but now his expression seems to change. His features relax, and while his voice varies, sometimes wrenched with pain, for the*

most part he seems removed from his dying. He
smiles)

Thank you, Peter. I mean that, now; thank you very much.
(PETER'S mouth drops open. He cannot move; he
is transfixed)

Oh, Peter, I was so afraid I'd drive you away. (He laughs
as best he can) You don't know how afraid I was you'd
go away and leave me. And now I'll tell you what happened at the zoo. I think . . . I think this is what happened at the zoo . . . I think. I think that while I was
at the zoo I decided that I would walk north . . . northerly, rather . . . until I found you . . . or somebody . . .
and I decided that I would talk to you . . . I would
tell you things . . . and things that I would tell you
would . . . Well, here we are. You see? Here we are.
But . . . I don't know . . . could I have planned all
this? No . . . no, I couldn't have. But I think I did. And
now I've told you what you wanted to know, haven't I?
And now you know all about what happened at the zoo.
And now you know what you'll see in your TV, and the
face I told you about . . . you remember . . . the face
I told you about . . . my face, the face you see right
now. Peter . . . Peter? . . . Peter . . . thank you. I
came unto you (He laughs, so faintly) and you have
comforted me. Dear Peter.

PETER

(Almost fainting) Oh my God!

JERRY

You'd better go now. Somebody might come by, and you
don't want to be here when anyone comes.

PETER

(Does not move, but begins to weep)
Oh my God, oh my God.

JERRY

(Most faintly, now; he is very near death)
You won't be coming back here any more, Peter; you've

been dispossessed. You've lost your bench, but you've defended your honor. And Peter, I'll tell you something now; you're not really a vegetable; it's all right, you're an animal. You're an animal, too. But you'd better hurry now, Peter. Hurry, you'd better go . . . see?

    (JERRY *takes a handkerchief and with great effort and pain wipes the knife handle clean of finger-prints*)

Hurry away, Peter.

    (PETER *begins to stagger away*)

Wait . . . wait, Peter. Take your book . . . book. Right here . . . beside me . . . on your bench . . . my bench, rather. Come . . . take your book.

    (PETER *starts for the book, but retreats*)

Hurry . . . Peter.

    (PETER *rushes to the bench, grabs the book, retreats*)

Very good, Peter . . . very good. Now . . . hurry away.

    (PETER *hesitates for a moment, then flees, stage-left*)

Hurry away. . . . (*His eyes are closed now*) Hurry away, your parakeets are making the dinner . . . the cats . . . are setting the table . . .

PETER (*Off stage*)
    (*A pitiful howl*)
OH MY GOD!

JERRY
    (*His eyes still closed, he shakes his head and speaks; a combination of scornful mimicry and supplication*)
Oh . . . my . . . God.
    (*He is dead*)

CURTAIN

The American Dream

A PLAY IN ONE SCENE (1959–1960)

For David Diamond

PREFACE

The comments by the Messers Watts, Balliett, and Taubman, printed at the end of this Preface, while they are representative of a majority of critical reaction to *The American Dream,* do not tell the whole story. Naturally not. No sensible publisher will tout opinions antagonistic to his product. And while I have, in my brief (three years, five plays—two of them but fifteen minutes long) and happy time as a playwright, received enough good press to last me a lifetime, I would like to concern myself, here, with some of the bad—not because I am a masochist, but because I would like to point up, foolhardy though it may be of me, what I consider to be a misuse of the critical function in American press letters.

For example: The off-Broadway critic for one of New York's morning tabloids had his sensibilities (or something) so offended by the *content* of *The American Dream* that he refused to review the next play of mine that opened.

Another example: A couple of other critics (Bright Gentlemen who do their opinions for Intellectualist Weekly Sheets of—sadly, all in all—very small circulation) went all to pieces over the (to their mind) nihilist, immoral, defeatist *content* of the play. And so on.

May I submit that when a critic sets himself up as an arbiter of morality, a judge of the matter and not the manner of a work, he is no longer a critic; he is a censor.

And just what is the *content* of *The American Dream* (a comedy, yet) that so upsets these guardians of the public morality? The play is an examination of the American Scene, an attack on the substitution of arti-

ficial for real values in our society, a condemnation of
complacency, cruelty, emasculation and vacuity; it is a
stand against the fiction that everything in this slipping
land of ours is peachy-keen.

Is the play offensive? I certainly hope so; it was my
intention to offend—as well as amuse and entertain.
Is it nihilist, immoral, defeatist? Well, to that let me answer that *The American Dream* is a picture of our time
—as I see it, of course. Every honest work is a personal,
private yowl, a statement of one individual's pleasure or
pain; but I hope that *The American Dream* is something
more than that. I hope that it transcends the personal
and the private, and has something to do with the an-
guish of us all.

EDWARD ALBEE

New York City
May 24, 1961

"If sheer creative talent appeals to you, I recommend
The American Dream. . . . It is packed with untamed
imagination, wild humor, gleefully sardonic satirical
implications, and overtones of strangely touching sadness, and I thought it was entirely delightful. . . . Mr.
Albee [is] a playwright of fresh and remarkable
talent."   —RICHARD WATTS, JR., *New York Post*

"*The American Dream* is a unique and often brilliant
play. Its horrible aspects, which reach directly back
to the butchery and perversion of the Greek theatre, are
forbidding, for they have nothing to do with a stage
business of moans and blood and bodies. Far worse, the
play's horror is only reported or implied, and it is further
pointed up by being juxtaposed with an unfailing and
wholly original comic inventiveness that is by turns ridiculous, satiric, sardonic, and sensibly Surrealistic. No
sooner has a Sophoclean dismemberment been mentioned
than it is illumined by a comic sense that matches and
often resembles the comic sense of Gertrude Stein,
Lewis Carroll, and Jacques Tati. The play is not realistic,

but neither is it purely illusory. It is, in the fashion of a comic nightmare, fantasy of the highest order. . . . This is a play for the resilient young and the wise old. All those paunchy, sluggish targets in between had best stay away." —WHITNEY BALLIETT, *The New Yorker*

"It is agreed that Edward Albee has talent. *The Zoo Story* . . . established that point. *The American Dream* . . . reinforces it. . . . Mr. Albee handles his chosen technique with a disarmingly childlike and sardonic freshness."

—HOWARD TAUBMAN, *The New York Times*

FIRST PERFORMANCE: January 24, 1961,

New York City. York Playhouse

The American Dream

The Players: MOMMY
               DADDY
               GRANDMA
               MRS. BARKER
               YOUNG MAN

The Scene:

A living room. Two armchairs, one toward either side of the stage, facing each other diagonally out toward the audience. Against the rear wall, a sofa. A door, leading out from the apartment, in the rear wall, far stage-right. An archway, leading to other rooms, in the side wall, stage-left.

At the beginning, MOMMY *and* DADDY *are seated in the armchairs,* DADDY *in the armchair stage-left,* MOMMY *in the other.*

Curtain up. A silence. Then:

MOMMY

I don't know what can be keeping them.

DADDY

They're late, naturally.

MOMMY

Of course, they're late; it never fails.

DADDY

That's the way things are today, and there's nothing you can do about it.

MOMMY

You're quite right.

DADDY

When we took this apartment, they were quick enough

57

to have me sign the lease; they were quick enough to take my check for two months' rent in advance . . .

MOMMY

And one month's security . . .

DADDY

. . . and one month's security. They were quick enough to check my references; they were quick enough about all that. But now! But now, try to get the icebox fixed, try to get the doorbell fixed, try to get the leak in the johnny fixed! Just try it . . . they aren't so quick about *that.*

MOMMY

Of course not; it never fails. People think they can get away with anything these days . . . and, of course they can. I went to buy a new hat yesterday.
(*Pause*)
I said, I went to buy a new hat yesterday.

DADDY

Oh! Yes . . . yes.

MOMMY

Pay attention.

DADDY

I *am* paying attention, Mommy.

MOMMY

Well, be sure you do.

DADDY

Oh, I am.

MOMMY

All right, Daddy; now listen.

DADDY

I'm listening, Mommy.

MOMMY

You're sure!

DADDY

Yes . . . yes, I'm sure, I'm all ears.

MOMMY
 (*Giggles at the thought; then*)
All right, now. I went to buy a new hat yesterday and I said, "I'd like a new hat, please." And so, they showed me a few hats, green ones and blue ones, and I didn't like any of them, not one bit. What did I say? What did I just say?

DADDY

You didn't like any of them, not one bit.

MOMMY

That's right; you just keep paying attention. And then they showed me one that I did like. It was a lovely little hat, and I said, "Oh, this is a lovely little hat; I'll take this hat; oh my, it's lovely. What color is it?" And they said, "Why, this is beige; isn't it a lovely little beige hat?" And I said, "Oh, it's just lovely." And so, I bought it.
 (*Stops, looks at* DADDY)

DADDY
 (*To show he is paying attention*)
And so you bought it.

MOMMY

And so I bought it, and I walked out of the store with the hat right on my head, and I ran spang into the chairman of our woman's club, and she said, "Oh, my dear, isn't that a lovely little hat? Where did you get that lovely little hat? It's the loveliest little hat; I've always wanted a wheat-colored hat *myself*." And, I said, "Why, no, my dear; this hat is beige; beige." And she laughed and said, "Why no, my dear, that's a wheat-colored hat . . . wheat. I know beige from wheat." And I said, "Well, my dear, I know beige from wheat, too." What did I say? What did I just say?

DADDY
(*Tonelessly*)
Well, my dear, I know beige from wheat, too.

MOMMY
That's right. And she laughed, and she said, "Well, my dear, they certainly put one over on you. That's wheat if I ever saw wheat. But it's lovely, just the same." And then she walked off. She's a dreadful woman, you don't know her; she has dreadful taste, two dreadful children, a dreadful house, and an absolutely adorable husband who sits in a wheel chair all the time. You don't know him. You don't know anybody, do you? She's just a dreadful woman, but she *is* chairman of our woman's club, so naturally I'm terribly fond of her. So, I went right back into the hat shop, and I said, "Look here; what do you mean selling me a hat that you say is beige, when it's wheat all the time . . . wheat! I can tell beige from wheat any day in the week, but not in this artificial light of yours." They have artificial light, Daddy.

DADDY
Have they!

MOMMY
And I said, "The minute I got outside I could tell that it wasn't a beige hat at all; it was a wheat hat." And they said to me, "How could you tell that when you had the hat on the top of your head?" Well, that made me angry, and so I made a scene right there; I screamed as hard as I could; I took my hat off and I threw it down on the counter, and oh, I made a terrible scene. I said, I made a terrible scene.

DADDY

(*Snapping to*)
Yes . . . yes . . . good for you!

MOMMY

And I made an absolutely terrible scene; and they became frightened, and they said, "Oh, madam; oh, madam." But I kept right on, and finally they admitted that they might have made a mistake; so they took my hat into the back, and then they came out again with a hat that looked exactly like it. I took one look at it, and I said, "This hat is wheat-colored; wheat." Well, of course, they said, "Oh, no, madam, this hat is beige; you go outside and see." So, I went outside, and lo and behold, it *was* beige. So I bought it.

DADDY

(*Clearing his throat*)
I would imagine that it was the same hat they tried to sell you before.

MOMMY

(*With a little laugh*)
Well, of course it was!

DADDY

That's the way things are today; you just can't get satisfaction; you just try.

MOMMY

Well, *I* got satisfaction.

DADDY

That's right, Mommy. *You did* get satisfaction, didn't you?

MOMMY

Why are they so late? I don't know what can be keeping them.

DADDY

I've been trying for two weeks to have the leak in the johnny fixed.

MOMMY

You can't get satisfaction; just try. *I* can get satisfaction, but you can't.

DADDY

I've been trying for two weeks and it isn't so much for my sake; I can always go to the club.

MOMMY

It isn't so much for my sake, either; I can always go shopping.

DADDY

It's really for Grandma's sake.

MOMMY

Of course it's for Grandma's sake. Grandma cries every time she goes to the johnny as it is; but now that it doesn't work it's even worse, it makes Grandma think she's getting feeble-headed.

DADDY

Grandma *is* getting feeble-headed.

MOMMY

Of course Grandma is getting feeble-headed, but not about her johnny-do's.

DADDY

No; that's true. I must have it fixed.

MOMMY

WHY are they so late? I don't know what can be keeping them.

DADDY

When they came here the first time, they were ten minutes early; they were quick enough about it then.

(*Enter* GRANDMA *from the archway, stage left.
She is loaded down with boxes, large and small,
neatly wrapped and tied.*)

MOMMY

Why Grandma, look at you! What *is* all that you're
carrying?

GRANDMA

They're boxes. What do they look like?

MOMMY

Daddy! Look at Grandma; look at all the boxes she's
carrying!

DADDY

My goodness, Grandma; look at all those boxes.

GRANDMA

Where'll I put them?

MOMMY

Heavens! I don't know. Whatever are they for?

GRANDMA

That's nobody's damn business.

MOMMY

Well, in that case, put them down next to Daddy; there.

GRANDMA

(*Dumping the boxes down, on and around*
DADDY'S *feet*)

I sure wish you'd get the john fixed.

DADDY

Oh, I do wish they'd come and fix it. We hear you . . . for hours . . . whimpering away. . . .

MOMMY

Daddy! What a terrible thing to say to Grandma!

GRANDMA

Yeah. For shame, talking to me that way.

DADDY

I'm sorry, Grandma.

MOMMY

Daddy's sorry, Grandma.

GRANDMA

Well, all right. In that case I'll go get the rest of the boxes. I suppose I deserve being talked to that way. I've gotten so old. Most people think that when you get so old, you either freeze to death, or you burn up. But you don't. When you get so old, all that happens is that people talk to you that way.

DADDY

(Contrite)
I said I'm sorry, Grandma.

MOMMY

Daddy said he was sorry.

GRANDMA

Well, that's all that counts. People being sorry. Makes you feel better; gives you a sense of dignity, and that's all that's important . . . a sense of dignity. And it doesn't matter if you don't care, or not, either. You got to have a sense of dignity, even if you don't care, 'cause, if you don't have that, civilization's doomed.

MOMMY

You've been reading my book club selections again!

DADDY

How dare you read Mommy's book club selections, Grandma!

GRANDMA

Because I'm old! When you're old you gotta do something. When you get old, you can't talk to people because people snap at you. When you get so old, people talk to you that way. That's why you become deaf, so you won't be able to hear people talking to you that way. And that's why you go and hide under the covers in the big soft bed, so you won't feel the house shaking from people talking to you that way. That's why old people die, eventually. People talk to them that way. I've got to go and get the rest of the boxes.

(GRANDMA *exits*)

DADDY

Poor Grandma, I didn't mean to hurt her.

MOMMY

Don't you worry about it; Grandma doesn't know what she means.

DADDY

She knows what she says, though.

MOMMY

Don't you worry about it; she won't know that soon. I love Grandma.

DADDY

I love her, too. Look how nicely she wrapped these boxes.

MOMMY

Grandma has always wrapped boxes nicely. When I was

a little girl, I was very poor, and Grandma was very poor, too, because Grandpa was in heaven. And every day, when I went to school, Grandma used to wrap a box for me, and I used to take it with me to school; and when it was lunchtime, all the little boys and girls used to take out their boxes of lunch, and they weren't wrapped nicely at all, and they used to open them and eat their chicken legs and chocolate cakes; and I used to say, "Oh, look at my lovely lunch box; it's so nicely wrapped it would break my heart to open it." And so, I wouldn't open it.

DADDY

Because it was empty.

MOMMY

Oh no. Grandma always filled it up, because she never ate the dinner she cooked the evening before; she gave me all her food for my lunch box the next day. After school, I'd take the box back to Grandma, and she'd open it and eat the chicken legs and chocolate cake that was inside. Grandma used to say, "I love day-old cake." That's where the expression day-old cake came from. Grandma always ate everything a day late. I used to eat all the other little boys' and girls' food at school, because they thought my lunch box was empty. They thought my lunch box was empty, and that's why I wouldn't open it. They thought I suffered from the sin of pride, and since that made them better than me, they were very generous.

DADDY

You were a very deceitful little girl.

MOMMY

We were very poor! But then I married you, Daddy, and now we're very rich.

DADDY

Grandma isn't rich.

MOMMY

No, but you've been so good to Grandma she feels rich. She doesn't know you'd like to put her in a nursing home.

DADDY

I wouldn't!

MOMMY

Well, heaven knows, *I* would! I can't stand it, watching her do the cooking and the housework, polishing the silver, moving the furniture. . . .

DADDY

She likes to do that. She says it's the least she can do to earn her keep.

MOMMY

Well, she's right. You can't live off people. I can live off you, because I married you. And aren't you lucky all I brought with me was Grandma. A lot of women I know would have brought their whole families to live off you. All I brought was Grandma. Grandma is all the family I have.

DADDY

I feel very fortunate.

MOMMY

You should. I have a right to live off of you because I married you, and because I used to let you get on top of me and bump your uglies; and I have a right to all your money when you die. And when you do, Grandma and I can live by ourselves . . . if she's still here. Unless you have her put away in a nursing home.

DADDY

I have no intention of putting her in a nursing home.

MOMMY

Well, I wish somebody would do something with her!

DADDY

At any rate, you're very well provided for.

MOMMY

You're my sweet Daddy; that's very nice.

DADDY

I love my Mommy.
          (*Enter* GRANDMA *again, laden with more boxes*)

GRANDMA

          (*Dumping the boxes on and around* DADDY's *feet*)
There; that's the lot of them.

DADDY

They're wrapped so nicely.

GRANDMA

          (*To* DADDY)
You won't get on my sweet side that way . . .

MOMMY

Grandma!

GRANDMA

. . . telling me how nicely I wrap boxes. Not after what
you said: how I whimpered for hours. . . .

MOMMY

Grandma!

GRANDMA

          (*To* MOMMY)
Shut up!
          (*To* DADDY)
You don't have any feelings, that's what's wrong with
you. Old people make all sorts of noises, half of them
they can't help. Old people whimper, and cry, and belch,
and make great hollow rumbling sounds at the table; old
people wake up in the middle of the night screaming,

and find out they haven't even been asleep; and when old people *are* asleep, they try to wake up, and they can't . . . not for the longest time.

MOMMY

Homilies, homilies!

GRANDMA

And there's more, too.

DADDY

I'm really very sorry, Grandma.

GRANDMA

I know you are, Daddy; it's Mommy over there makes all the trouble. If you'd listened to me; you wouldn't have married her in the first place. She was a tramp and a trollop and a trull to boot, and she's no better now.

MOMMY

Grandma!

GRANDMA

(*To* MOMMY)

Shut up!

(*To* DADDY)

When she was no more than eight years old she used to climb up on my lap and say, in a sickening little voice, "When I gwo up, I'm going to mahwy a wich old man; I'm going to set my wittle were end right down in a tub o' butter, that's what I'm going to do." And I warned you, Daddy; I told you to stay away from her type. I told you to. I did.

MOMMY

You stop that! You're my mother, not his!

GRANDMA

I am?

DADDY

That's right, Grandma. Mommy's right.

GRANDMA

Well, how would you expect somebody as old as I am to remember a thing like that? You don't make allowances for people. I want an allowance. I want an allowance!

DADDY

All right, Grandma; I'll see to it.

MOMMY

Grandma! I'm ashamed of you.

GRANDMA

Humf! It's a fine time to say that. You should have gotten rid of me a long time ago if that's the way you feel. You should have had Daddy set me up in business somewhere . . . I could have gone into the fur business, or I could have been a singer. But no; not you. You wanted me around so you could sleep in my room when Daddy got fresh. But now it isn't important, because Daddy doesn't want to get fresh with you any more, and I don't blame him. You'd rather sleep with me, wouldn't you, Daddy?

MOMMY

Daddy doesn't want to sleep with anyone. Daddy's been sick.

DADDY

I've been sick. I don't even want to sleep in the apartment.

MOMMY

You see? I told you.

DADDY

I just want to get everything over with.

MOMMY

That's right. Why are they so late? Why can't they get here on time?

GRANDMA

(*An owl*)

Who? Who? ... Who? Who?

MOMMY

You know, Grandma.

GRANDMA

No, I don't.

MOMMY

Well, it doesn't really matter whether you do or not.

DADDY

Is that true?

MOMMY

Oh, more or less. Look how pretty Grandma wrapped these boxes.

GRANDMA

I didn't really like wrapping them; it hurt my fingers, and it frightened me. But it had to be done.

MOMMY

Why, Grandma?

GRANDMA

None of your damn business.

MOMMY

Go to bed.

GRANDMA

I don't want to go to bed. I just got up. I want to stay here and watch. Besides ...

MOMMY

Go to bed.

DADDY

Let her stay up, Mommy; it isn't noon yet.

GRANDMA

I want to watch; besides . . .

DADDY

Let her watch, Mommy.

MOMMY

Well all right, you can watch; but don't you dare say a word.

GRANDMA

Old people are very good at listening; old people don't like to talk; old people have colitis and lavender perfume. Now I'm going to be quiet.

DADDY

She never mentioned she wanted to be a singer.

MOMMY

Oh, I forgot to tell you, but it was ages ago.
      (*The doorbell rings*)
Oh, goodness! Here they are!

GRANDMA

Who? Who?

MOMMY

Oh, just some people.

GRANDMA

The van people? Is it the van people? Have you finally done it? Have you called the van people to come and take me away?

DADDY

Of course not, Grandma!

GRANDMA

Oh, don't be too sure. She'd have you carted off too, if she thought she could get away with it.

MOMMY

Pay no attention to her, Daddy.
(*An aside to* GRANDMA)

My God, you're ungrateful!
(*The doorbell rings again*)

DADDY
(*Wringing his hands*)
Oh dear; oh dear.

MOMMY
(*Still to* GRANDMA)
Just you wait; I'll fix your wagon.
(*Now to* DADDY)
Well, go let them in Daddy. What are you waiting for?

DADDY

I think we should talk about it some more. Maybe we've been hasty . . . a little hasty, perhaps.
(*Doorbell rings again*)
I'd like to talk about it some more.

MOMMY

There's no need. You made up your mind; you were firm; you were masculine and decisive.

DADDY

We might consider the pros and the . . .

MOMMY

I won't argue with you; it has to be done; you were right. Open the door.

DADDY

But I'm not sure that . . .

MOMMY

Open the door.

DADDY

Was I firm about it?

MOMMY

Oh, so firm; so firm.

DADDY

And was I decisive?

MOMMY

SO decisive! Oh, I shivered.

DADDY

And masculine? Was I really masculine?

MOMMY

Oh, Daddy, you were so masculine; I shivered and fainted.

GRANDMA

Shivered and fainted, did she? Humf!

MOMMY

You be quiet.

GRANDMA

Old people have a right to talk to themselves; it doesn't hurt the gums, and it's comforting.
  (*Doorbell rings again*)

DADDY

I shall now open the door.

MOMMY

WHAT a masculine Daddy! Isn't he a masculine Daddy?

GRANDMA

Don't expect me to say anything. Old people are obscene.

MOMMY

Some of your opinions aren't so bad. You know that?

DADDY
(*Backing off from the door*)
Maybe we can send them away.

MOMMY

Oh, look at you! You're turning into jelly; you're inde-
cisive; you're a woman.

DADDY

All right. Watch me now; I'm going to open the door.
Watch. Watch!

MOMMY

We're watching; we're watching.

GRANDMA

I'm not.

DADDY

Watch now; it's opening.
(*He opens the door*)
It's open!
(MRS. BARKER *steps into the room*)
Here they are!

MOMMY

Here they are!

GRANDMA

Where?

DADDY

Come in. You're late. But, of course, we expected you to
be late; we were saying that we expected you to be late.

MOMMY

Daddy, don't be rude! We were saying that you just can't get satisfaction these days, and we were talking about you, of course. Won't you come in?

MRS. BARKER

Thank you. I don't mind if I do.

MOMMY

We're very glad that you're here, late as you are. You do remember us, don't you? You were here once before. I'm Mommy, and this is Daddy, and that's Grandma, doddering there in the corner.

MRS. BARKER

Hello, Mommy; hello, Daddy; and hello there, Grandma.

DADDY

Now that you're here, I don't suppose you could go away and maybe come back some other time.

MRS. BARKER

Oh no; we're much too efficient for that. I said, hello there, Grandma.

MOMMY

Speak to them, Grandma.

GRANDMA

I don't see them.

DADDY

For shame, Grandma; they're here.

MRS. BARKER

Yes, we're here, Grandma. I'm Mrs. Barker. I remember you; don't you remember me?

GRANDMA

I don't recall. Maybe you were younger, or something.

MOMMY

Grandma! What a terrible thing to say!

MRS. BARKER

Oh now, don't scold her, Mommy; for all she knows she may be right.

DADDY

Uh . . . Mrs. Barker, is it? Won't you sit down?

MRS. BARKER

I don't mind if I do.

MOMMY

Would you like a cigarette, and a drink, and would you like to cross your legs?

MRS. BARKER

You forget yourself, Mommy; I'm a professional woman. But I will cross my legs.

DADDY

Yes, make yourself comfortable.

MRS. BARKER

I don't mind if I do.

GRANDMA

Are they still here?

MOMMY

Be quiet, Grandma.

MRS. BARKER

Oh, we're still here. My, what an unattractive apartment you have!

MOMMY

Yes, but you don't know what a trouble it is. Let me tell you . . .

DADDY

I was saying to Mommy . . .

MRS. BARKER

Yes, I know. I was listening outside.

DADDY

About the icebox, and . . . the doorbell . . . and the . . .

MRS. BARKER

. . . and the johnny. Yes, we're very efficient; we have to know everything in our work.

DADDY

Exactly what do you do?

MOMMY

Yes, what is your work?

MRS. BARKER

Well, my dear, for one thing, I'm chairman of your woman's club.

MOMMY

Don't be ridiculous. I was talking to the chairman of my woman's club just yester— Why, so you are. You remember, Daddy, the lady I was telling you about? The lady with the husband who sits in the *swing?* Don't you remember?

DADDY

No . . . no. . . .

MOMMY

Of course you do. I'm so sorry, Mrs. Barker. I would have known you anywhere, except in this artificial light. And look! You have a hat just like the one I bought yesterday.

MRS. BARKER
(*With a little laugh*)
No, not really; this hat is cream.

MOMMY
Well, my dear, that may look like a cream hat to you, but
I can . . .

MRS. BARKER
Now, now; you seem to forget who I am.

MOMMY
Yes, I do, don't I? Are you sure you're comfortable?
Won't you take off your dress?

MRS. BARKER
I don't mind if I do.
(*She removes her dress*)

MOMMY
There. You must feel a great deal more comfortable.

MRS. BARKER
Well, I certainly *look* a great deal more comfortable.

DADDY
I'm going to blush and giggle.

MOMMY
Daddy's going to blush and giggle.

MRS. BARKER
(*Pulling the hem of her slip above her knees*)
You're lucky to have such a man for a husband.

MOMMY
Oh, don't I know it!

DADDY
I just blushed and giggled and went sticky wet.

MOMMY

Isn't Daddy a caution, Mrs. Barker?

MRS. BARKER

Maybe if I smoked . . . ?

MOMMY

Oh, that isn't necessary.

MRS. BARKER

I don't mind if I do.

MOMMY

No; no, don't. Really.

MRS. BARKER

I don't mind . . .

MOMMY

I won't have you smoking in my house, and that's that!
You're a professional woman.

DADDY

Grandma drinks AND smokes; don't you, Grandma?

GRANDMA

No.

MOMMY

Well, now, Mrs. Barker; suppose you tell us why you're
here.

GRANDMA

(As MOMMY *walks through the boxes*)
The boxes . . . the boxes . . .

MOMMY

Be quiet, Grandma.

DADDY

What did you say, Grandma?

GRANDMA

(*As* MOMMY *steps on several of the boxes*)
The boxes, damn it!

MRS. BARKER

Boxes; she said boxes. She mentioned the boxes.

DADDY

What about the boxes, Grandma? Maybe Mrs. Barker
is here because of the boxes. Is that what you meant,
Grandma?

GRANDMA

I don't know if that's what I meant or not. It's certainly
not what I *thought* I meant.

DADDY

Grandma is of the opinion that . . .

MRS. BARKER

Can we assume that the boxes are for us? I mean, can
we assume that you had us come here for the boxes?

MOMMY

Are you in the habit of receiving boxes?

DADDY

A very good question.

MRS. BARKER

Well, that would depend on the reason we're here. I've
got my fingers in so many little pies, you know. Now,
I can think of one of my little activities in which we are
in the habit of receiving *baskets;* but more in a literary
sense than really. We *might* receive boxes, though, under very special circumstances. I'm afraid that's the best
answer I can give you.

DADDY

It's a very interesting answer.

MRS. BARKER

I thought so. But, does it help?

MOMMY

No; I'm afraid not.

DADDY

I wonder if it might help us any if I said I feel misgivings, that I have definite qualms.

MOMMY

Where, Daddy?

DADDY

Well, mostly right here, right around where the stitches were.

MOMMY

Daddy had an operation, you know.

MRS. BARKER

Oh, you poor Daddy! I didn't know; but then, how could I?

GRANDMA

You might have asked; it wouldn't have hurt you.

MOMMY

Dry up, Grandma.

GRANDMA

There you go. Letting your true feelings come out. Old people aren't dry enough, I suppose. My sacks are empty, the fluid in my eyeballs is all caked on the inside edges, my spine is made of sugar candy, I breathe ice; but you don't hear me complain. Nobody hears old people complain because people think that's all old people do. And

that's because old people are gnarled and sagged and twisted into the shape of a complaint.
> (*Signs off*)

That's all.

MRS. BARKER

What was wrong, Daddy?

DADDY

Well, you know how it is: the doctors took out something that was there and put in something that wasn't there. An operation.

MRS. BARKER

You're very fortunate, I should say.

MOMMY

Oh, he is; he is. All his life, Daddy has wanted to be a United States Senator; but now . . . why now he's changed his mind, and for the rest of his life he's going to want to be Governor . . . it would be nearer the apartment, you know.

MRS. BARKER

You *are* fortunate, Daddy.

DADDY

Yes, indeed; except that I get these qualms now and then, definite ones.

MRS. BARKER

Well, it's just a matter of things settling; you're like an old house.

MOMMY

Why Daddy, thank Mrs. Barker.

DADDY

Thank you.

MRS. BARKER

Ambition! That's the ticket. I have a brother who's very much like you, Daddy . . . ambitious. Of course, he's a great deal younger than you; he's even younger than I am . . . if such a thing is possible. He runs a little newspaper. Just a little newspaper . . . but he runs it. He's chief cook and bottle washer of that little newspaper, which he calls *The Village Idiot*. He has such a sense of humor; he's so self-deprecating, so modest. And he'd never admit it himself, but he *is* the Village Idiot.

MOMMY

Oh, I think that's just grand. Don't you think so, Daddy?

DADDY

Yes, just grand.

MRS. BARKER

My brother's a dear man, and he has a dear little wife, whom he loves, dearly. He loves her so much he just can't get a sentence out without mentioning her. He wants everybody to know he's married. He's really a stickler on that point; he can't be introduced to anybody and say hello without adding, "Of course, I'm married." As far as I'm concerned, he's the chief exponent of Woman Love in this whole country; he's even been written up in psychiatric journals because of it.

DADDY

Indeed!

MOMMY

Isn't that lovely.

MRS. BARKER

Oh, I think so. There's too much woman hatred in this country, and that's a fact.

GRANDMA

Oh, I don't know.

MOMMY

Oh, I think that's just grand. Don't you think so, Daddy?

DADDY

Yes, just grand.

GRANDMA

In case anybody's interested . . .

MOMMY

Be quiet, Grandma.

GRANDMA

Nuts!

MOMMY

Oh, Mrs. Barker, you *must* forgive Grandma. She's rural.

MRS. BARKER

I don't mind if I do.

DADDY

Maybe Grandma has something to say.

MOMMY

Nonsense. Old people have nothing to say; and if old
people *did* have something to say, nobody would listen
to them.
        (*To* GRANDMA)
You see? I can pull that stuff just as easy as you can.

GRANDMA

Well, you got the rhythm, but you don't really have the
quality. Besides, you're middle-aged.

MOMMY

I'm proud of it!

GRANDMA

Look. I'll show you how it's really done. Middle-aged

people think they can do anything, but the truth is that middle-aged people can't do most things as well as they used to. Middle-aged people think they're special because they're like everybody else. We live in the age of deformity. You see? Rhythm *and* content. You'll learn

. DADDY

I do wish I weren't surrounded by women; I'd like some men around here.

MRS. BARKER

You can say that again!

GRANDMA

I don't hardly count as a woman, so can I say my piece?

MOMMY

Go on. Jabber away.

GRANDMA

It's very simple; the fact is, these boxes don't have anything to do with why this good lady is come to call. Now, if you're interested in knowing why these boxes *are* here . . .

DADDY

I'm sure that must be all very true, Grandma, but what does it have to do with why . . . pardon me, what is that name again?

MRS. BARKER

Mrs. Barker.

DADDY

Exactly. What does it have to do with why . . . that name again?

MRS. BARKER

Mrs. Barker.

DADDY

Precisely. What does it have to do with why what's-her-name is here?

MOMMY

They're here because we asked them.

MRS. BARKER

Yes. That's why.

GRANDMA

Now if you're interested in knowing why these boxes *are* here . . .

MOMMY

Well, nobody *is* interested!

GRANDMA

You can be as snippety as you like for all the good it'll do you.

DADDY

You two will have to stop arguing.

MOMMY

I don't argue with her.

DADDY

It will just have to stop.

MOMMY

Well, why don't you call a van and have her taken away?

GRANDMA

Don't bother; there's no need.

DADDY

No, now, perhaps I can go away myself. . . .

MOMMY

Well, one or the other; the way things are now it's impossible. In the first place, it's too crowded in this apartment.

(*To* GRANDMA)

And it's you that takes up all the space, with your enema bottles, and your Pekinese, and God-only-knows-what-else . . . and now all these boxes. . . .

GRANDMA

These boxes are . . .

MRS. BARKER

I've never heard of enema *bottles*. . . .

GRANDMA

She means enema bags, but she doesn't know the difference. Mommy comes from extremely bad stock. And besides, when Mommy was born . . . well, it was a difficult delivery, and she had a head shaped like a banana.

MOMMY

You ungrateful— Daddy? Daddy, you see how ungrateful she is after all these years, after all the things we've done for her?

(*To* GRANDMA)

One of these days you're going away in a van; that's what's going to happen to you!

GRANDMA

Do tell!

MRS. BARKER

Like a banana?

GRANDMA

Yup, just like a banana.

MRS. BARKER

My word!

MOMMY

You stop listening to her; she'll say anything. Just the other night she called Daddy a hedgehog.

MRS. BARKER

She didn't!

GRANDMA

That's right, baby; you stick up for me.

MOMMY

I don't know where she gets the words; on the television, maybe.

MRS. BARKER

Did you really call him a hedgehog?

GRANDMA

Oh look; what difference does it make whether I did or not?

DADDY

Grandma's right. Leave Grandma alone.

MOMMY

(*To* DADDY)
How dare you!

GRANDMA

Oh, leave her alone, Daddy; the kid's all mixed up.

MOMMY

You see? I told you. It's all those television shows. Daddy, you go right into Grandma's room and take her television and shake all the tubes loose.

DADDY

Don't mention tubes to me.

MOMMY

Oh! Mommy forgot!
(*To* MRS. BARKER)
Daddy has tubes now, where he used to have tracts.

MRS. BARKER

Is that a fact!

GRANDMA

I know why this dear lady is here.

MOMMY

You be still.

MRS. BARKER

Oh, I do wish you'd tell me.

MOMMY

No! No! That wouldn't be fair at all.

DADDY

Besides, she knows why she's here; she's here because
we called them.

MRS. BARKER

La! But that still leaves me puzzled. I know I'm here
because you called us, but I'm such a busy girl, with this
committee and that committee, and the Responsible
Citizens Activities I indulge in.

MOMMY

Oh my; busy, busy.

MRS. BARKER

Yes, indeed. So I'm afraid you'll have to give me some
help.

MOMMY

Oh, no. No, you must be mistaken. I can't believe we
asked you here to give you any help. With the way taxes

are these days, and the way you can't get satisfaction in ANYTHING . . . no, I don't believe so.

DADDY

And if you need help . . . why, I should think you'd apply for a Fulbright Scholarship. . . .

MOMMY

And if not that . . . why, then a Guggenheim Fellowship. . . .

GRANDMA

Oh, come on; why not shoot the works and try for the Prix de Rome.
(*Under her breath to* MOMMY *and* DADDY)
Beasts!

MRS. BARKER

Oh, what a jolly family. But let me think. I'm knee-deep in work these days; there's the Ladies' Auxiliary Air Raid Committee, for one thing; how do you feel about air raids?

MOMMY

Oh, I'd say we're hostile.

DADDY

Yes, definitely; we're hostile.

MRS. BARKER

Then, you'll be no help there. There's too much hostility in the world these days as it is; but I'll not badger you! There's a surfeit of badgers as well.

GRANDMA

While we're at it, there's been a run on old people, too. The Department of Agriculture, or maybe it wasn't the Department of Agriculture—anyway, it was some department that's run by a girl—put out figures showing that ninety per cent of the adult population of the coun-

try is over eighty years old . . . or eighty per cent is
over ninety years old . . .

MOMMY

You're such a liar! You just finished saying that everyone is middle-aged.

GRANDMA

I'm just telling you what the government says . . . that
doesn't have anything to do with what . . .

MOMMY

It's that television! Daddy, go break her television.

GRANDMA

You won't find it.

DADDY
          (*Wearily getting up*)
If I must . . . I must.

MOMMY

And don't step on the Pekinese; it's blind.

DADDY

It may be blind, but Daddy isn't.
          (*He exits, through the archway, stage left*)

GRANDMA

You won't find *it*, either.

MOMMY

Oh, I'm so fortunate to have such a husband. Just think;
I could have a husband who was poor, or argumentative,
or a husband who sat in a wheel chair all day . . .
OOOOHHHH! *What* have I said? What *have* I said?

GRANDMA

You said you could have a husband who sat in a
wheel . . .

MOMMY

I'm mortified! I could die! I could cut my tongue out! I could . . .

MRS. BARKER
(*Forcing a smile*)
Oh, now . . . now . . . don't think about it . . .

MOMMY

I could . . . why, I could . . .

MRS. BARKER
. . . don't think about it . . . really. . . .

MOMMY

You're quite right. I won't think about it, and that way I'll forget that I ever said it, and that way it will be all right.
(*Pause*)
There . . . I've forgotten. Well, now, now that Daddy is out of the room we can have some girl talk.

MRS. BARKER

I'm not sure that I . . .

MOMMY

You *do* want to have some girl talk, don't you?

MRS. BARKER

I was going to say I'm not sure that I wouldn't care for a glass of water. I feel a little faint.

MOMMY

Grandma, go get Mrs. Barker a glass of water.

GRANDMA

Go get it yourself. I quit.

MOMMY

Grandma loves to do little things around the house; it gives her a false sense of security.

GRANDMA

I quit! I'm through!

MOMMY

Now, you be a good Grandma, or you know what will happen to you. You'll be taken away in a van.

GRANDMA

You don't frighten me. I'm too old to be frightened. Besides . . .

MOMMY

WELL! I'll tend to you later. I'll hide your teeth . . . I'll . . .

GRANDMA

Everything's hidden.

MRS. BARKER

I *am* going to faint. I *am*.

MOMMY

Good heavens! I'll go myself.
          (*As she exits, through the archway, stage-left*)
I'll fix you, Grandma. I'll take care of you later.
          (*She exits*)

GRANDMA

Oh, go soak your head.
          (*To* MRS. BARKER)
Well, dearie, how do you feel?

MRS. BARKER

A little better, I think. Yes, much better, thank you, Grandma.

GRANDMA

That's good.

MRS. BARKER

But . . . I feel so lost . . . not knowing why I'm here
. . . and, on top of it, they say I was here before.

GRANDMA

Well, you were. You weren't *here*, exactly, because
we've moved around a lot, from one apartment to another, up and down the social ladder like mice, if you
like similes.

MRS. BARKER

I don't . . . particularly.

GRANDMA

Well, then, I'm sorry.

MRS. BARKER

(*Suddenly*)
Grandma, I feel I can trust you.

GRANDMA

Don't be too sure; it's every man for himself around this
place. . . .

MRS. BARKER

Oh . . . is it? Nonetheless, I really do feel that I can
trust you. *Please* tell me why they called and asked us to
come. I implore you!

GRANDMA

Oh my; that feels good. It's been so long since anybody
implored me. Do it again. Implore me some more.

MRS. BARKER

You're your daughter's mother, all right!

GRANDMA

Oh, I don't mean to be hard. If you won't implore me, then beg me, or ask me, or entreat me . . . just anything like that.

MRS. BARKER

You're a dreadful old woman!

GRANDMA

You'll understand some day. Please!

MRS. BARKER

Oh, for heaven's sake! . . . I implore you . . . I beg you . . . I beseech you!

GRANDMA

Beseech! Oh, that's the nicest word I've heard in ages. You're a dear, sweet woman. . . . You . . . beseech . . . me. I can't resist that.

MRS. BARKER

Well, then . . . please tell me why they asked us to come.

GRANDMA

Well, I'll give you a hint. That's the best I can do, because I'm a muddleheaded old woman. Now listen, because it's important. Once upon a time, not too very long ago, but a long enough time ago . . . oh, about twenty years ago . . . there was a man very much like Daddy, and a woman very much like Mommy, who were married to each other, very much like Mommy and Daddy are married to each other; and they lived in an apartment very much like one that's very much like this one, and they lived there with an old woman who was very much like yours truly, only younger, because it was some time ago; in fact, they were all somewhat younger.

MRS. BARKER

How fascinating!

GRANDMA

Now, at the same time, there was a dear lady very much
like you, only younger then, who did all sorts of Good
Works. . . . And one of the Good Works this dear lady
did was in something very much like a volunteer capacity
for an organization very much like the Bye-Bye Adoption Service, which is nearby and which was run by a
terribly deaf old lady very much like the Miss Bye-Bye
who runs the Bye-Bye Adoption Service nearby.

MRS. BARKER

How enthralling!

GRANDMA

Well, be that as it may. Nonetheless, one afternoon this
man, who was very much like Daddy, and this woman
who was very much like Mommy came to see this dear
lady who did all the Good Works, who was very much
like you, dear, and they were very sad and very hopeful,
and they cried and smiled and bit their fingers, and they
said all the most intimate things.

MRS. BARKER

How spellbinding! What did they say?

GRANDMA

Well, it was very sweet. The woman, who was very much
like Mommy, said that she and the man who was very
much like Daddy had never been blessed with anything
very much like a bumble of joy.

MRS. BARKER

A what?

GRANDMA

A bumble; a bumble of joy.

MRS. BARKER

Oh, like bundle.

GRANDMA

Well, yes; very much like it. Bundle, bumble; who cares?
At any rate, the woman, who was very much like
Mommy, said that they wanted a bumble of their own,
but that the man, who was very much like Daddy,
couldn't have a bumble; and the man, who was very
much like Daddy, said that yes, they had wanted a
bumble of their own, but that the woman, who was very
much like Mommy, couldn't have one, and that now
they wanted to buy something very much like a bumble.

MRS. BARKER

How engrossing!

GRANDMA

Yes. And the dear lady, who was very much like you,
said something that was very much like, "Oh, what a
shame; but take heart . . . I think we have just the
bumble *for* you." And, well, the lady, who was very
much like Mommy, and the man, who was very much
like Daddy, cried and smiled and bit their fingers, and
said some more intimate things, which were totally ir-
relevant but which were pretty hot stuff, and so the
dear lady, who was very much like you, and who had
something very much like a penchant for pornography,
listened with something very much like enthusiasm.
"Whee," she said. "Whoooopeeeeee!" But that's beside
the point.

MRS. BARKER

I suppose *so*. But how gripping!

GRANDMA

Anyway . . . they *bought* something very much like a
bumble, and they took it away with them. But . . .
things didn't work out very well.

MRS. BARKER

You mean there was trouble?

GRANDMA

You got it.

(*With a glance through the archway*)

But, I'm going to have to speed up now because I think I'm leaving soon.

MRS. BARKER

Oh. Are you really?

GRANDMA

Yup.

MRS. BARKER

But old people don't go anywhere; they're either taken places, or put places.

GRANDMA

Well, this old person is different. Anyway . . . things started going badly.

MRS. BARKER

Oh yes. Yes.

GRANDMA

Weeeeellll . . . in the first place, it turned out the bumble didn't look like either one of its parents. That was enough of a blow, but things got worse. One night, it cried its heart out, if you can imagine such a thing.

MRS. BARKER

Cried its heart out! Well!

GRANDMA

But that was only the beginning. Then it turned out it only had eyes for its Daddy.

MRS. BARKER

For its Daddy! Why, any self-respecting woman would have gouged those eyes right out of its head.

GRANDMA

Well, she did. That's exactly what she did. But then, it kept its nose up in the air.

MRS. BARKER

Ufggh! How disgusting!

GRANDMA

That's what they thought. But *then,* it began to develop an interest in its you-know-what.

MRS. BARKER

In its you-know-what! Well! I hope they cut its hands off at the wrists!

GRANDMA

Well, yes, they did that eventually. But first, they cut off its you-know-what.

MRS. BARKER

A much better idea!

GRANDMA

That's what they thought. But after they cut off its you-know-what, it *still* put its hands under the covers, *looking* for its you-know-what. So, finally, they *had* to cut off its hands at the wrists.

MRS. BARKER

Naturally!

GRANDMA

And it was such a resentful bumble. Why, one day it called its Mommy a dirty name.

MRS. BARKER

Well, I hope they cut its tongue out!

GRANDMA

Of course. And then, as it got bigger, they found out

all sorts of terrible things about it, like: it didn't have a head on its shoulders, it had no guts, it was spineless, its feet were made of clay . . . just dreadful things.

MRS. BARKER

Dreadful!

GRANDMA

So you can understand how they became discouraged.

MRS. BARKER

I certainly can! And what did they do?

GRANDMA

What did they do? Well, for the last straw, it finally up and died; and you can imagine how *that* made them feel, their having paid for it, and all. So, they called up the lady who sold them the bumble in the first place and told her to come right over to their apartment. They wanted satisfaction; they wanted their money back. That's what they wanted.

MRS. BARKER

My, my, my.

GRANDMA

How do you like *them* apples?

MRS. BARKER

My, my, my.

DADDY

(*Off stage*)

Mommy! I can't find Grandma's television, and I can't find the Pekinese, either.

MOMMY

(*Off stage*)

Isn't that funny! And I can't find the water.

GRANDMA

Heh, heh, heh. I told them everything was hidden.

MRS. BARKER

Did you hide the water, too?

GRANDMA

(*Puzzled*)
No. No, I didn't do *that*.

DADDY

(*Off stage*)
The truth of the matter is, I can't even find Grandma's room.

GRANDMA

Heh, heh, heh.

MRS. BARKER

My! You certainly did hide things, didn't you?

GRANDMA

Sure, kid, sure.

MOMMY

(*Sticking her head in the room*)
Did you ever hear of such a thing, Grandma? Daddy can't find your television, and he can't find the Pekinese, and the truth of the matter is he can't even find your room.

GRANDMA

I told you. I hid everything.

MOMMY

Nonsense, Grandma! Just wait until I get my hands on you. You're a troublemaker . . . that's what you are.

GRANDMA

Well, I'll be out of here pretty soon, baby.

MOMMY

Oh, you don't know how right you are! Daddy's been wanting to send you away for a long time now, but I've been restraining him. I'll tell you one thing, though . . . I'm getting sick and tired of this fighting, and I might just let him have his way. Then you'll see what'll happen. Away you'll go; in a van, too. I'll let Daddy call the van man.

GRANDMA

I'm way ahead of you.

MOMMY

How can you be so old and so smug at the same time? You have no sense of proportion.

GRANDMA

You just answered your own question.

MOMMY

Mrs. Barker, I'd much rather you came into the kitchen for that glass of water, what with Grandma out here, and all.

MRS. BARKER

I don't see what Grandma has to do with it; and besides, I don't think you're very polite.

MOMMY

You seem to forget that you're a guest in this house . . .

GRANDMA

Apartment!

MOMMY

Apartment! And that you're a professional woman. So, if you'll be so good as to come into the kitchen, I'll be more than happy to show you where the water is, and where the glass is, and then you can put two and two together, if you're clever enough.

(*She vanishes*)

MRS. BARKER

(*After a moment's consideration*)

I suppose she's right.

GRANDMA

Well, that's how it is when people call you up and ask you over to do something for them.

MRS. BARKER

I suppose you're right, too. Well, Grandma, it's been very nice talking to you.

GRANDMA

And I've enjoyed listening. Say, don't tell Mommy or Daddy that I gave you that hint, will you?

MRS. BARKER

Oh, dear me, the hint! I'd forgotten about it, if you can imagine such a thing. No, I won't breathe a word of it to them.

GRANDMA

I don't know if it helped you any . . .

MRS. BARKER

I can't tell, yet. I'll have to . . . what *is* the word I want? . . . I'll have to relate it . . . that's it . . . I'll have to relate it to certain things that I *know,* and . . . draw . . . conclusions. . . . What I'll really have to do is to see if it applies to anything. I mean, after all, I *do* do volunteer work for an adoption service, but it isn't very much *like* the Bye-Bye Adoption Service . . . it *is* the Bye-Bye Adoption Service . . . and while I can remember Mommy and Daddy coming to see me, oh, about twenty years ago, about buying a bumble, I can't quite remember anyone very much *like* Mommy and Daddy coming to see me about buying a bumble. Don't you see? It really presents quite a problem. . . . I'll have to think about it . . . mull it . . . but at any rate, it was truly first-class of you to try to help me. Oh, will you still be here after I've had my drink of water?

GRANDMA

Probably . . . I'm not as spry as I used to be.

MRS. BARKER

Oh. Well, I won't say good-by then.

GRANDMA

No. Don't.
(MRS. BARKER *exits through the archway*)
People don't say good-by to old people because they think they'll frighten them. Lordy! If they only knew how awful "hello" and "my, you're looking chipper" sounded, they wouldn't say those things either. The truth is, there isn't much you *can* say to old people that doesn't sound just terrible.
(*The doorbell rings*)
Come on in!
(*The* YOUNG MAN *enters.* GRANDMA *looks him over*)
Well, now, aren't you a breath of fresh air!

YOUNG MAN

Hello there.

GRANDMA

My, my, my. Are you the van man?

YOUNG MAN

The what?

GRANDMA

The van man. The van man. Are you come to take me away?

YOUNG MAN

I don't know what you're talking about.

GRANDMA

Oh.
    (*Pause*)
Well.
    (*Pause*)
My, my, aren't you something!

YOUNG MAN

Hm?

GRANDMA

I said, my, my, aren't you something.

YOUNG MAN

Oh. Thank you.

GRANDMA

You don't sound very enthusiastic.

YOUNG MAN

Oh, I'm . . . I'm used to it.

GRANDMA

Yup . . . yup. You know, if I were about a hundred and fifty years younger I could go for you.

YOUNG MAN

Yes, I imagine so.

GRANDMA

Unh-hunh . . . will you look at those muscles!

YOUNG MAN
    (*Flexing his muscles*)
Yes, they're quite good, aren't they?

GRANDMA

Boy, they sure are. They natural?

YOUNG MAN

Well the basic structure was there, but I've done some work, too . . . you know, in a gym.

GRANDMA

I'll bet you have. You ought to be in the movies, boy.

YOUNG MAN

I know.

GRANDMA

Yup! Right up there on the old silver screen. But I suppose you've heard that before.

YOUNG MAN

Yes, I have.

GRANDMA

You ought to try out for them . . . the movies.

YOUNG MAN

Well, actually, I may have a career there yet. I've lived out on the West Coast almost all my life . . . and I've met a few people who . . . might be able to help me. I'm not in too much of a hurry, though. I'm almost as young as I look.

GRANDMA

Oh, that's nice. And will you look at that face!

YOUNG MAN

Yes, it's quite good, isn't it? Clean-cut, midwest farm boy type, almost insultingly good-looking in a typically American way. Good profile, straight nose, honest eyes, wonderful smile . . .

GRANDMA

Yup. Boy, you know what you are, don't you? You're the American Dream, that's what you are. All those other people, they don't know what they're talking about. You ... *you* are the American Dream.

YOUNG MAN

Thanks.

MOMMY
(*Off stage*)
Who rang the doorbell?

GRANDMA
(*Shouting off-stage*)
The American Dream!

MOMMY
(*Off stage*)
What? What was that, Grandma?

GRANDMA
(*Shouting*)
The American Dream! The American Dream! Damn it!

DADDY
(*Off stage*)
How's that, Mommy?

MOMMY
(*Off stage*)
Oh, some gibberish; pay no attention. Did you find Grandma's room?

DADDY
(*Off stage*)
No. I can't even find Mrs. Barker.

YOUNG MAN

What was all that?

GRANDMA

Oh, that was just the folks, but let's not talk about them, honey; let's talk about you.

YOUNG MAN

All right.

GRANDMA

Well, let's see. If you're not the van man, what are you doing here?

YOUNG MAN

I'm looking for work.

GRANDMA

Are you! Well, what kind of work?

YOUNG MAN

Oh, almost anything . . . almost anything that pays. I'll do almost anything for money.

GRANDMA

Will you . . . will you? Hmmmm. I wonder if there's anything you could do around here?

YOUNG MAN

There might be. It looked to be a likely building.

GRANDMA

It's always looked to be a rather unlikely building to me, but I suppose you'd know better than I.

YOUNG MAN

I can sense these things.

GRANDMA

There *might* be something you could do around here. Stay there! Don't come any closer.

YOUNG MAN

Sorry.

GRANDMA

I don't mean I'd *mind*. I don't know whether I'd mind,
or not. . . . But it wouldn't look well; it would look just
awful.

YOUNG MAN

Yes; I suppose so.

GRANDMA

Now, stay there, let me concentrate. What could you
do? The folks have been in something of a quandary
around here today, sort of a dilemma, and I wonder if
you mightn't be some help.

YOUNG MAN

I hope so . . . if there's money in it. Do you have any
money?

GRANDMA

Money! Oh, there's more money around here than you'd
know what to do with.

YOUNG MAN

I'm not so sure.

GRANDMA

Well, maybe not. Besides, I've got money of my own.

YOUNG MAN

You have?

GRANDMA

Sure. Old people quite often have lots of money; more
often than most people expect. Come here, so I can
whisper to you . . . not too close. I might faint.

YOUNG MAN

Oh, I'm sorry.

GRANDMA

It's all right, dear. Anyway . . . have you ever heard of that big baking contest they run? The one where all the ladies get together in a big barn and bake away?

YOUNG MAN

I'm . . . not . . . sure. . . .

GRANDMA

Not so close. Well, it doesn't matter whether you've heard of it or not. The important thing is—and I don't want anybody to hear this . . . the folks think I haven't been out of the house in eight years—the important thing is that I won first prize in that baking contest this year. Oh, it was in all the papers; not under my own name, though. I used a *nom de boulangère;* I called myself Uncle Henry.

YOUNG MAN

Did you?

GRANDMA

Why not? I didn't see any reason not to. I look just as much like an old man as I do like an old woman. And you know what I called it . . . what I won for?

YOUNG MAN

No. What did you call it?

GRANDMA

I called it Uncle Henry's Day-Old Cake.

YOUNG MAN

That's a very nice name.

GRANDMA

And it wasn't any trouble, either. All I did was go out

and get a store-bought cake, and keep it around for a while, and then slip it in, unbeknownst to anybody. Simple.

YOUNG MAN

You're a very resourceful person.

GRANDMA

Pioneer stock.

YOUNG MAN

Is all this true? Do you want me to believe all this?

GRANDMA

Well, you can believe it or not . . . it doesn't make any difference to me. All *I* know is, Uncle Henry's Day-Old Cake won me twenty-five thousand smackerolas.

YOUNG MAN

Twenty-five thou—

GRANDMA

Right on the old loggerhead. Now . . . how do you like them apples?

YOUNG MAN

Love 'em.

GRANDMA

I thought you'd be impressed.

YOUNG MAN

Money talks.

GRANDMA

Hey! You look familiar.

YOUNG MAN

Hm? Pardon?

GRANDMA

I said, you look familiar.

YOUNG MAN

Well, I've done some modeling.

GRANDMA

No . . . no. I don't mean that. You look familiar.

YOUNG MAN

Well, I'm a type.

GRANDMA

Yup; you sure are. Why do you say you'd do anything for money . . . if you don't mind my being nosy?

YOUNG MAN

No, no. It's part of the interviews. I'll be happy to tell you. It's that I have no talents at all, except what you see . . . my person; my body, my face. In every other way I am incomplete, and I must therefore . . . compensate.

GRANDMA

What do you mean, incomplete? You look pretty complete to me.

YOUNG MAN

I think I can explain it to you, partially because you're very old, and very old people have perceptions they keep to themselves, because if they expose them to other people . . . well, you know what ridicule and neglect are.

GRANDMA

I do, child, I do.

YOUNG MAN

Then listen. My mother died the night that I was born,

and I never knew my father; I doubt my mother did. But, I wasn't alone, because lying with me . . . in the placenta . . . there was someone else . . . my brother . . . my twin.

GRANDMA

Oh, my child.

YOUNG MAN

We were identical twins . . . he and I . . . not fraternal . . . identical; we were derived from the same ovum; and in *this,* in that we were twins not from separate ova but from the same one, we had a kinship such as you cannot imagine. We . . . we felt each other breathe . . . his heartbeats thundered in my temples . . . mine in his . . . our stomachs ached and we cried for feeding at the same time . . . are you old enough to understand?

GRANDMA

I think so, child; I think I'm nearly old enough.

YOUNG MAN

I hope so. But we were separated when we were still very young, my brother, my twin and I . . . inasmuch as you can separate one being. We were torn apart . . . thrown to opposite ends of the continent. I don't know what became of my brother . . . to the rest of myself . . . except that, from time to time, in the years that have passed, I have suffered losses . . . that I can't explain. A fall from grace . . . a departure of innocence . . . loss . . . loss. How can I put it to you? All right; like this: Once . . . it was as if all at once my heart . . . became numb . . . almost as though I . . . almost as though . . . just like that . . . it had been wrenched from my body . . . and from that time I have been unable to love. Once . . . I was asleep at the time . . . I awoke, and my eyes were burning. And since that time I have been unable to see anything, *anything,* with pity, with affection . . . with anything but . . . cool disinterest. And my groin . . . even there . . . since one time . . . one specific agony . . . since then I have not been able to *love* anyone with my body. And even my hands . . . I cannot touch another person and feel love. And there is more . . . there are more losses, but it all comes down to this: I no longer have the capacity to feel anything. I have no emotions. I have been drained, torn asunder . . . disemboweled. I have, now, only my person . . . my body, my face. I use what I have . . . I let people love me . . . I accept the syntax around me, for while I know I cannot relate . . . I know I must be related *to*. I let people love me . . . I let people touch me . . . I let them draw pleasure from my groin . . . from my presence . . . from the fact of me . . . but, that is all it comes to. As I told you, I am incomplete . . . I can feel nothing. I can feel nothing. And so . . . here I am . . . as you see me. I am . . . but this . . . what you see. And it will always be thus.

faith of society

illusion

GRANDMA

Oh, my child; my child.

(*Long pause; then*)

I was mistaken . . . before. I don't know you from somewhere, but I knew . . . once . . . someone very much like you . . . or, very much as perhaps you were.

YOUNG MAN

Be careful; be very careful. What I have told you may not be true. In my profession . . .

GRANDMA

Shhhhhh.

(*The* YOUNG MAN *bows his head, in acquiescence*)

Someone . . . to be more precise . . . who might have turned out to be very much like you might have turned out to be. And . . . unless I'm terribly mistaken . . . you've found yourself a job.

YOUNG MAN

What are my duties?

MRS. BARKER
(*Off stage*)
Yoo-hoo! Yoo-hoo!

GRANDMA

Oh-oh. You'll . . . you'll have to play it by ear, my dear
. . . unless I get a chance to talk to you again. I've got
to go into my act, now.

YOUNG MAN

But, I . . .

GRANDMA

Yoo-hoo!

MRS. BARKER
(*Coming through archway*)
Yoo-hoo . . . . oh, there you are, Grandma. I'm glad to
see somebody. I can't find Mommy or Daddy.
(*Double takes*)
Well . . . who's this?

GRANDMA

This? Well . . . un . . . oh, this is the . . . uh . . . the
van man. That's who it is . . . the van man.

MRS. BARKER

So! It's true! They *did* call the van man. They *are* having you carted away.

GRANDMA
(*Shrugging*)
Well, you know. It figures.

MRS. BARKER
(*To* YOUNG MAN)
How dare you cart this poor old woman away!

YOUNG MAN
(*After a quick look at* GRANDMA, *who nods*)
I do what I'm paid to do. I don't ask any questions.

MRS. BARKER
(*After a brief pause*)
Oh.
(*Pause*)
Well, you're quite right, of course, and I shouldn't meddle.

GRANDMA
(*To* YOUNG MAN)
Dear, will you take my things out to the van?
(*She points to the boxes*)

YOUNG MAN
(*After only the briefest hesitation*)
Why certainly.

GRANDMA
(*As the* YOUNG MAN *takes up half the boxes, exits by the front door*)
Isn't that a nice young van man?

MRS. BARKER
(*Shaking her head in disbelief, watching the* YOUNG MAN *exit*)
Unh-hunh . . . some things have changed for the better. I remember when I had *my* mother carted off . . . the van man who came for her wasn't anything near as nice as this one.

GRANDMA
Oh, did you have your mother carted off, too?

MRS. BARKER
(*Cheerfully*)
Why certainly! Didn't you?

GRANDMA
(*Puzzling*)
No . . . no, I didn't. At least, I can't remember. Listen dear; I got to talk to you for a second.

MRS. BARKER
Why certainly, Grandma.

GRANDMA
Now, listen.

MRS. BARKER
Yes, Grandma. Yes.

GRANDMA
Now listen carefully. You got this dilemma here with Mommy and Daddy . . .

MRS. BARKER
Yes! I wonder where they've gone to?

GRANDMA
They'll be back in. Now, LISTEN!

MRS. BARKER
Oh, I'm sorry.

GRANDMA
Now, you got this dilemma here with Mommy and Daddy, and I think I got the way out for you.
(*The* YOUNG MAN *re-enters through the front door*)
Will you take the rest of my things out now, dear?
(*To* MRS. BARKER, *while the* YOUNG MAN *takes the rest of the boxes, exits again by the front door*)
Fine. Now listen, dear.
(*She begins to whisper in* MRS. BARKER'*s ear*)

MRS. BARKER

Oh! Oh! Oh! I don't think I could . . . do you really think I could? Well, why not? What a wonderful idea . . . what an absolutely wonderful idea!

GRANDMA

Well, yes, I thought it was.

MRS. BARKER

And you so old!

GRANDMA

Heh, heh, heh. ·

MRS. BARKER

Well, I think it's absolutely marvelous, anyway. I'm going to find Mommy and Daddy right now.

GRANDMA

Good. You do that.

MRS. BARKER

Well, now. I think I will say good-by. I can't thank you enough.
      (*She starts to exit through the archway*)

GRANDMA

You're welcome. Say it!

MRS. BARKER

Huh? What?

GRANDMA

Say good-by.

MRS. BARKER

Oh. Good-by.
      (*She exits*)
Mommy! I say, Mommy! Daddy!

GRANDMA

Good-by.
>*(By herself now, she looks about)*

Ah me.
>*(Shakes her head)*

Ah me.
>*(Takes in the room)*

Good-by.
>*(The YOUNG MAN re-enters)*

GRANDMA

Oh, hello, there.

YOUNG MAN

All the boxes are outside.

GRANDMA

>*(A little sadly)*

I don't know why I bother to take them with me. They don't have much in them . . . some old letters, a couple of regrets . . . Pekinese . . . blind at that . . . the television . . . my Sunday teeth . . . eighty-six years of living . . . some sounds . . . a few images, a little garbled by now . . . and, well . . .
>*(She shrugs)*

. . . you know . . . the things one accumulates.

YOUNG MAN

Can I get you . . . a cab, or something?

GRANDMA

Oh no, dear . . . thank you just the same. I'll take it from here.

YOUNG MAN

And what shall I do now?

GRANDMA

Oh, you stay here, dear. It will all become clear to you. It will be explained. You'll understand.

YOUNG MAN

Very well.

GRANDMA
(*After one more look about*)

Well ...

YOUNG MAN

Let me see you to the elevator.

GRANDMA

Oh ... that *would* be nice, dear.
(*They both exit by the front door, slowly*)

(*Enter* MRS. BARKER, *followed by* MOMMY *and* DADDY)

MRS. BARKER

... and I'm happy to tell you that the whole thing's settled. Just like that.

MOMMY

Oh, we're so glad. We were afraid there might be a problem, what with delays, and all.

DADDY

Yes, we're very relieved.

MRS. BARKER

Well, now; that's what professional women are for.

MOMMY

Why . . . where's Grandma? Grandma's not here! Where's Grandma? And look! The boxes are gone, too. Grandma's gone, and so are the boxes. She's taken off, and she's stolen something! Daddy!

MRS. BARKER

Why, Mommy, the van man was here.

MOMMY

(*Startled*)

The what?

MRS. BARKER

The van man. The van man was here.

(*The lights might dim a little, suddenly*)

MOMMY

(*Shakes her head*)

No, that's impossible.

MRS. BARKER

Why, I saw him with my own two eyes.

MOMMY

(*Near tears*)

No, no, that's impossible. No. There's no such thing as the van man. There is no van man. We . . . we made him up. Grandma? Grandma?

DADDY

(*Moving to* MOMMY)

There, there, now.

MOMMY

Oh Daddy . . . where's Grandma?

DADDY

There, there, now.

(*While* DADDY *is comforting* MOMMY, GRANDMA *comes out, stage right, near the footlights*)

GRANDMA

(*To the audience*)

Shhhhhh! I want to watch this.

(*She motions to* MRS. BARKER *who, with a secret smile, tiptoes to the front door and opens it. The* YOUNG MAN *is framed therein. Lights up full again as he steps into the room*)

MRS. BARKER

Surprise! Surprise! Here we are!

MOMMY

What? What?

DADDY

Hm? What?

MOMMY
(*Her tears merely sniffles now*)
What surprise?

MRS. BARKER

Why, I told you. The surprise I told you about.

DADDY

You ... you know, Mommy.

MOMMY

Sur ... prise?

DADDY
(*Urging her to cheerfulness*)
You remember, Mommy; why we asked ... uh ...
what's-her-name to come here?

MRS. BARKER

Mrs. Barker, if you don't mind.

DADDY

Yes. Mommy? You remember now? About the bumble
... about wanting satisfaction?

MOMMY
(*Her sorrow turning into delight*)
Yes. Why yes! Of course! Yes! Oh, how wonderful!

MRS. BARKER
(*To the* YOUNG MAN)
This is Mommy.

YOUNG MAN
How . . . how do you do?

MRS. BARKER
(*Stage whisper*)
Her name's Mommy.

YOUNG MAN
How . . . how do you do, Mommy?

MOMMY
Well! Hello there!

MRS. BARKER
(*To the* YOUNG MAN)
And that is Daddy.

YOUNG MAN
How do you do, sir?

DADDY
How do you do?

MOMMY
(*Herself again, circling the* YOUNG MAN, *feeling his arm, poking him*)
Yes, sir! Yes, sirree! Now this is more like it. Now this is a great deal more like it! Daddy! Come see. Come see if this isn't a great deal more like it.

DADDY
I . . . I can see from here, Mommy. It does look a great deal more like it.

MOMMY

Yes, sir. Yes sirree! Mrs. Barker, I don't know *how* to thank you.

MRS. BARKER

Oh, don't worry about that. I'll send you a bill in the mail.

MOMMY

What this really calls for is a celebration. It calls for a drink.

MRS. BARKER

Oh, what a nice idea.

MOMMY

There's some sauterne in the kitchen.

YOUNG MAN

I'll go.

MOMMY

Will you? Oh, how nice. The kitchen's through the arch-way there.
    (*As the* YOUNG MAN *exits: to* MRS. BARKER)
He's very nice. Really top notch; much better than the other one.

MRS. BARKER

I'm glad you're pleased. And I'm glad everything's all straightened out.

MOMMY

Well, at least we know why we sent for you. We're glad that's cleared up. By the way, what's his name?

MRS. BARKER

Ha! Call him whatever you like. He's yours. Call him what you called the other one.

MOMMY

Daddy? What did we call the other one?

DADDY
        (*Puzzles*)
Why . . .

YOUNG MAN
        (*Re-entering with a tray on which are a bottle of
        sauterne and five glasses*)
Here we are!

MOMMY

Hooray! Hooray!

MRS. BARKER

Oh, good!

MOMMY
        (*Moving to the tray*)
So, let's— Five glasses? Why five? There are only four
of us. Why five?

YOUNG MAN
        (*Catches* GRANDMA's *eye;* GRANDMA *indicates she
        is not there*)
Oh, I'm sorry.

MOMMY

You must learn to count. We're a wealthy family, and
you must learn to count.

YOUNG MAN

I will.

MOMMY

Well, everybody take a glass.
        (*They do*)
And we'll drink to celebrate. To satisfaction! Who says
you can't get satisfaction these days!

MRS. BARKER

What dreadful sauterne!

MOMMY

Yes, isn't it?

(*To* YOUNG MAN, *her voice already a little fuzzy from the wine*)

You don't know how happy I am to see you! Yes sirree. Listen, that time we had with . . . with the other one. I'll tell you about it some time.

(*Indicates* MRS. BARKER)

After she's gone. She was responsible for all the trouble in the first place. I'll tell you all about it.

(*Sidles up to him a little*)

Maybe . . . maybe later tonight.

YOUNG MAN

(*Not moving away*)

Why yes. That would be very nice.

MOMMY

(*Puzzles*)

Something familiar about you . . . you know that? I can't quite place it. . . .

GRANDMA

(*Interrupting . . . to audience*)

Well, I guess that just about wraps it up. I mean, for better or worse, this is a comedy, and I don't think we'd better go any further. No, definitely not. So, let's leave things as they are right now . . . while everybody's happy . . . while everybody's got what he wants . . . or everybody's got what he thinks he wants. Good night, dears.

CURTAIN

Other SIGNET Plays